MORE PRAISE FO[R] ...

"David Nicholson, and all those people I mentioned to you: You should talk to them. Really, go talk to them. Get a book out about them. Find a way to cultivate a larger audience for them."

—James Alan McPherson, Pulitzer Prize–winning author of *Elbow Room*

"In *Flying Home*, David Nicholson, the dauntless founder of *Black Film Review*, gives us a series of absorbing stories, captured for the reader in a linguistical version of CinemaScope, along with a most playful riff on Ralph Ellison's narrative style. Intimate yet wide-angled, imaginative and probing, Nicholson's collection is, as its last tale reveals, full of the inspiration and longing that come with having seen Hendrix perform live on the grandest of stages when music and society were on the edge of revolution."

—Henry Louis Gates Jr., Alphonse Fletcher University Professor, Harvard University

"David Nicholson, like his literary ancestors Ralph Ellison, James Alan McPherson, and Bernard Malamud, illuminates the mythic in the everyday lives of Americans whose stories are all too rarely deemed worthy of art... In *Flying Home*, David Nicholson shines his compassion and wisdom on them all."

—Eileen Pollack, author of *In the Mouth* and *Breaking and Entering*

"David Nicholson's *Flying Home*, a debut collection of seven stories, is simply astonishing. Nicholson probes deeply into black lives, and lives of the poor—and the professional—and shows us that they matter and how. Dialogue and dialect are spot on, the weather tangible, sentences as taut and vibrant as guitar strings, characters so real a reader feels enriched by and even responsible for their situations (we are all our brothers' keepers). I recommend this as a book to read, to lend, to teach, and to return to; it is beautifully written."

—Kelly Cherry, author of *A Kind of Dream: Stories*

"David Nicholson writes with subtle insight, vividly rendered, into the human condition. *Flying Home* is an accomplished book of stories that take us behind the curtains of race and class that separate us and often hide our common humanity."

—ARNOLD RAMPERSAD, author of *Ralph Ellison: A Biography*

"*Flying Home* is not elegiac, for there's too much love and humor and landscape in this fine collection about the often-hidden heart of the city. The people are real, and the place is vivid."

—SUSAN STRAIGHT, author of *A Million Nightingales* and *Highwire Moon*, a finalist for the National Book Award

"*Flying Home* is a collection of wonderful short stories. Nicholson writes like an elder watching a city change and knowing the difference between life and death. There is sweet goodness in these tales. Wisdom can be found in this book too. 'Seasons' is a baseball story I fell in love with. 'Flying Home' made me want to hug my daughter again—like it was fifteen years ago. As Washington slow dances with gentrification it's good to know a way of life has not been erased. Yes, the barbershop is open and friends still give rides to those who no longer know how to fly."

—E. ETHELBERT MILLER

"Sad, wise, funny, and forty other things, reading any one of David's stories is like watching a crystal form in front of your eyes: all the elements are there at once but the way they find each other, the connections made and the meanings forged, is genuinely impressive."

—MIKE LANKFORD, author of *Life in Double Time: Confessions of an American Drummer*

"David Nicholson's collection of stories is powerful, lyrical, and poignant—they slide into your soul and stay there. These stories spoke to my heart, and haven't quite left me."

—SARA J. HENRY, award-winning author of *A Cold and Lonely Place*

FLYING HOME

FLYING HOME

seven stories of the secret city

DAVID NICHOLSON

First edition.

ISBN-10: 0-931181-45-3
ISBN-13: 978-0-931181-45-0

"Among the Righteous" appeared in *Fiction 86* and in *Best Stories from New Writers*. "Carolina Is Dancing" first appeared in the *High Plains Literary Review*. "A Few Good Men" appeared in *Stress City: A Big Book of Fiction by 51 DC Guys* and in *Best African American Fiction 2010*. "Saving Jimi Hendrix" first appeared in *Kiss the Sky*.

Cover photo: Ron Roberson
Author image, back page: Richard Thompson
Book and cover design: Nita Congress
Printed by Main Street Rag Publishing, Charlotte, NC

Paycock Press
3819 North 13th Street
Arlington, VA 22201
http://www.gargoylemagazine.com

For Ruth
(these songs, because she could not sing them)

And for Liz and for Andrew and the grace of
second chances

But now, he thought, they would never see him;

for they believed that they had seen him already.

That was the hard part."

earl lovelace, the dragon can't dance

CONTENTS

GETTIN' ON THE GOOD FOOT

"August is the month when undone summer things must be finished or regretted all through the winter."

james alan mcpherson

rare summer mornings when it's still cool and the street of narrow brick houses quiet and empty, there's a quality to the light that makes the air almost palpable. Halfway down the cracked concrete steps to run an errand for his mother, Neville stands transfixed. It's like looking up from the bottom of a pool of clear, pristine water. Later, the heat will become almost audible, a soft, whirring insect whine, and only those with someplace to go—or no place at all—will brave the afternoon. Sounds will seem to come from far away, dim voices from radio or television, fragments of conversation, a child crying, a screen door slamming. But now, heartbeats before the rude slam of a screen door disturbs the morning stillness, the liquid air makes the world new again. Joined side by side, rooms stacked up one over the other and topped with pyramidal slate roofs, the Street's narrow houses are nothing like the houses in Freeport that spill from the hillsides steep with mango and banana trees, bright yellow, pink, and emerald stucco houses, one story with high ceilings and cool tile floors, wide doors that open from verandah to living room to kitchen to allow the ocean breeze. The dull, sickening ache of missing Freeport never quite goes away. But for a few moments on mornings like these, Neville can almost believe this street might truly one day be home.

living on the Street's like walking into the Sylvan after the picture's started. Neville knows he'll never really understand what he's watching because he's missed all the important stuff. But at the movies, he can sit through the intermission, the cartoon, and the newsreel to see the picture again. He can't do that on the Street. That's too bad, because just when he thinks he's started to understand, it throws him a curve—something he's heard Mr. Odom talk about in the barbershop that he thinks must be like the googly he was learning to throw when he still played cricket.

This time, it's a poster on the wall of the laundromat near Star-Brite Liquor where his father works evenings and Saturdays. Underneath the block letters THE HOWARD THEATER PRESENTS is a grainy photograph of a man with a broad, dimpled face and glossy, piled-high, straightened hair. He's bent over, microphone fisted in one hand, face contorted, eyes brash and knowing, as if he's waiting for you to find out what he's long since made his own. The man is James Brown; Neville knows this because his name is splashed in red ink surrounded by stars. Below are the words "Papa's Got a Brand New Bag."

Neville scowls, looking furtively up the Street for witnesses to his confusion. In a little while, Big Boy Bullock and the rest will claim the corner near the Avenue, squatting by their red Radio Flyers with the varnished wood sides, waiting for women like Miss Odessa Adelaide and Mrs. 'Lina Bledsoe who have no sons and are too old to carry their groceries home. But the corner's empty now, and the Street has a sleepy, Saturday-morning feel. Inside the laundromat, a stout woman in pink curlers peers out suspiciously before she turns to feed coins into a dryer. Across the street Mr. Lamarr Jenkins sits in a barber chair, turning the pages of a magazine while he listens to classical music on his console hi-fi. He'll tune to one of the soul stations, WOL or WOOK, before he turns the closed sign in the window.

Neville looks once more at the poster and turns away when it's clear James Brown won't give up his secret before Big Boy comes, not hurrying, but not taking his time about it either, as he makes his way towards the Safeway for the eggs, milk, and bread his mother has sent him to get, one more thing to figure out that he does not understand.

muttering savagely as she works, Mrs. 'Lina Bledsoe sweeps the walk in her backyard that's almost small enough for her to touch the fence on either side with outstretched hands. She wears an old housecoat whose flower pattern has faded to gauzy illegibility, stockings rolled just below her knees, shapeless slippers. Her hair, covered by an old cutoff stocking, is done up in finger-length gray braids. The yard is a riot of roses, day lilies, black-eyed Susans, and peonies. Honeysuckle covers the six-foot chain link fence. The roses are in full bloom, and the ground beneath the peach tree in the center of the yard is littered with pink blossoms.

Like a squall off Freeport, Mrs. Bledsoe can erupt at any time, provoked by public slight or private grievance into rages that can be vented only with shouts and curses, the sense of the words disappeared into inarticulate sound. Sometimes, the squall becomes a hurricane and she rages for days.

She's run down to a low mutter now, a steady grumble that, except for the occasional sharp swear word, might almost be a song she's humming. Leaning her broom against the fence, Mrs. Bledsoe bends to examine a rosebush. She snaps off a dead stem, tosses it onto a small pile of twigs, weeds, and faded blossoms before she goes to a green can of Ballantine Ale on the wooden porch steps. Using the opener she keeps on a nail hammered into the post, she punches two holes in the top. She drinks and takes a package of unfiltered Chesterfields and a silver Zippo lighter from the sagging pocket of her housecoat.

"Sometimes I don't know if it's worth it," she mutters, exhaling dragon-plumes as she studies the peach tree. "Ragged little urchins hopped the fence and stole damn near every piece of fruit last summer. Little black imps." She says it again, savoring the words like the taste of the ale or the draw of acrid smoke. "Little black imps. Stole damn near every last peach."

Though her house is on the same side of the alley—but perpendicular; the front's around the corner—Mrs. Bledsoe's voice is only a low background mutter to Neville upstairs in his room reading *The Adventures of Tom Sawyer* for the third time. His parents have the big room at the front of the house. The back room, his room, is far enough away so that he only hears them late at night when the Street's quiet. They argue the way they argued before his American grandfather's death showed his mother a way to leave the island. Months later, his father followed. Sometimes Neville wonders if it's something he's done that they're waiting for him to discover so he'll stop, but if he closes his door, he can hardly hear them at all.

He's laughing to himself at how easily Tom gets the other boys to whitewash the fence when he hears a short sharp whistle—his friend, Wilson, who comes over most Saturdays. And then Mrs. Bledsoe screeching, "Get away from that fence. Peaches ain't even ripe yet, and here you come—"

Neville hurries down the backstairs and into the kitchen, out the back door. Wilson's already over the fence and dropping down into the backyard. Before school ended for summer, Wilson came to the front door and rang the bell. Now Wilson's afraid to. Big Boy might see him.

"It's only Wilson," Neville starts. "Mr. Renfro's son. You've seen us out here playing ball."

While Wilson slinks towards the porch, Mrs. Bledsoe hooks her fingers in the chain link fence, looking at Neville head cocked as if sussing out a lie. There's a mole on her chin with a hair growing from it. Her breath's pungent with ale. Neville wants to look away, but Mrs. Bledsoe holds him with her gaze.

"You know that little rascal just went in your house," she says. "Better go make sure he ain't stealin'."

"But it's Wilson," Neville says. "He comes over almost every Saturday. Unless," he adds, "Mrs. Renfro's got something for him to do."

"Your momma and daddy know?"

"Yes, ma'am," he says, but Mrs. Bledsoe doesn't say, All right, or even, Go make sure everything's okay inside, just looks at him as she lights a cigarette and inhales. She coughs, rich and throaty.

"Hot ain't it?" she says. "Won't be nothin' like what it'll be come August, though. You'll see."

Neville thinks about telling Mrs. Bledsoe it gets hot in Freeport too, hotter than the Street and the Avenue because Freeport's nearer the equator, but he knows to let her go on till she loses interest or runs down.

"It's two things about summertime," Mrs. Bledsoe says, voice low and confiding, as if letting him in on a secret, "and that's niggers and heat. The two go together, just like shit 'n' flies. Niggers draw heat, but they can't stand it—makes 'em crazy. Come August, heat gets to 'em and they go crazy. Arguing and fighting, hootin' and hollerin', and here come those ragged little urchins, hell-bent on stealin' my peaches."

A wracking cough doubles her over and Mrs. Bledsoe hawks and spits before she presses her face against the fence, eying Neville shrewdly.

"Will you keep a lookout?" she says. "Can I count on you? I know my peaches'll be safe with you protectin' 'em from those thievin' little imps 'cause you're a good boy, Neville. You're a good boy."

"don't say nothin'," Wilson warns as Neville comes into the kitchen. "It ain't you Big Boy after."

"I wasn't going to," Neville protests, though he wants to ask why Wilson doesn't just talk to Big Boy. He wants to ask, too, who James Brown is and why the bag's brand new, but Wilson's looking hungrily at the bread he's left out. He asks if Wilson wants to eat. Wilson says, "Naw, I'm okay," and then, "You got any peanut butter? And some milk?"

Wilson makes the sandwich. But before Neville can get to his questions, he says indistinctly between bites, "You don't understand, see. Big Boy crazy. They say his momma hadda carry him up here 'cause he broke a teacher's jaw when the teacher try take him to the principal's office. Shoot—you so bad, you go find Big Boy and take up for me."

Neville shakes his head, remembering Big Boy stalking the playground as if he owned it, trailing a wake of girls' adoring gazes. He's unpredictable, as likely to greet you with a punch as a cheerful "Whass happenin'?"

He's taller than the other boys, broad across the chest, with the faint beginnings of a mustache across his lip. Held back twice, he was released to junior high school with the rest of Mrs. Berenethea Syphax's sixth-grade class only because the rules wouldn't allow him to be kept back again. In June, the day before promotion exercises, patience exhausted when he stuttered, mired in his two-line recitation, Mrs. Syphax pushed Big Boy to the back of the chorus. "Just move your lips without saying anything," she hissed, and gave Big Boy's part to Neville, making Neville the master of ceremonies and the only one with three speaking roles. Lurching back to his seat shamefaced, Big Boy mouthed threats. And then he saw Wilson's cartoon, himself holding an upside-down book, question marks penciled over his head. "Somebody gon' git a' ass-whuppin'," he promised. So far, Wilson's been spared, but only because his older brother, Wallace, is almost as tall as Big Boy.

they're watching cartoons on television, putting off deciding whether to go to the double feature at the Sylvan later, and risk Wilson running into Big Boy, when the bedroom door opens overhead. The toilet flushes, and then Neville's father comes downstairs, eyes red and heavy, cheeks stubbled with gray, barefoot in pajama bottoms. The springy hair on his bare chest has started to go gray too.

"Oh," Ivan says, a note of disappointment in his voice, as if he'd hoped for someone else. "It's you, Wilson."

He sits on the sofa, staring at the pictures on the mantel over the fireplace. There are a few from Freeport—himself alone in a suit on the verandah of the house in the country where he grew up, Naomi holding Neville when he was a baby. There's the one Neville's grandfather took in the backyard the day Ivan and Naomi were married. They're holding hands in front of the wooden fence that was there before the chain link, Naomi smiling shyly. She's taken off her glasses, or perhaps she'd not worn them that day. She looks sweet and innocent and girlish. Ivan wears his uniform, and he looks straight at the camera, grinning as if he's got everything in the world he wants.

Beside it's another picture of Ivan, a photograph in a silver frame. He's front and center, squatting with a group of men before an airplane. The words "Sweet Naomi" are painted in flowing script on the nose, above and behind the jet intake. Like the other men in the photograph, Ivan wears a leather jacket with a fur collar. His cap's pushed back on his head.

Studying himself, Ivan smiles sourly, despair rising from him as palpable as acrid sweat.

"This damn country," he says softly. "Gi' dem two years me life fightin' their damn war, and what it get me?"

Neville pretends to be engrossed in the old black-and-white cartoon, but it doesn't matter; the question requires no answer. His exaggerated laugh, designed to insulate himself from his father's unhappiness, prompts Ivan away from the picture. When Ivan chuckles, Neville looks up, smiling till he realizes there's nothing to share because his father wasn't watching.

"Boy," Ivan says, the broad "a" of the islands making it "Bwaayh." "You changin' right before me eyes. I lyin' upstairs listening, and I can't tell which onea you talkin'. You sounding like a regular little American."

Though he's aware of Wilson beside him on the floor, the rickety-tick music and soundtrack's sproinging sound effects, Neville doesn't look to see if Wilson's listening to his father. It's at times like these he feels his differentness, like the Chinese girl he read about in a book his mother brought home from the library. Her parents kept her grandmother's ashes in a vase on a shelf.

"You remember the shop?" his father asks.

Neville nods. It's only been six months; of course he remembers. There was a scale with a round, glass-faced dial that hung from a beam in the ceiling. He liked to watch the Indian shopkeeper pour sugar or salt or flour onto a square of brown paper on the scale's curved metal tray, then form the paper into a thick, brown cylinder, tuck-fastened at both ends.

"And you remember the old woman used to sit outside by the road?"

Again Neville nods. She was a stout woman, old, impossible to tell how old, dressed in voluminous faded patterned skirts, her head topped by a red bandanna. A patched cloth spread in front of her was covered with fruits and vegetables—ackee, mango, soursop, oranges, tangerines—and straw hats and straw dolls. A small pipe hung from her mouth, clenched in the space between missing teeth. She kept a fire burning beside the cloth to roast yams and ears of corn. Once, Neville had seen her pluck out a coal between thumb and forefinger to light the pipe.

"It just come to me to think about her," Ivan says. "I remember one time you t'ree, four years old and suppose to be taking a nap, you mother go to you room and you gone. Everybody raise one whole heap of fuss—the maid say somebody must kidnap you while she boiling the wash. You mother don't know what to do, so she call me at the office. I come straight home, but meanwhile somebody think to look down the road. And there you are, sitting beside the old lady, the two of you talk, talk, talking.

"The heat come up fierce fierce, man, and all me want to do is eat me dinner and leave back for work. But you mek me stan' there listening that old woman. She talk thick, thick country, and I can only make out one of every other word. But you, you understand everyt'ing she say, and me no have no idea what in the world the two of you talking about."

Wilson laughs in a way that shows it's a grown-up's story he doesn't really understand, but Neville's smile is wistful. He wants to say he remembers, and not just because it's important to his father. When he isn't working at Star-Brite, his father sits shirtless in the living room, watching television with the sound off, trying to reconcile himself to his new life. If he could remember, it might mean everything they'd had in Freeport wasn't really gone. But it is and like his father, Neville knows he'll never be the same. Something will replace what each of them has lost; it has to. But he has yet to find out what that will be, and the way to finding it means having to learn everything important all over again.

where the house-fronts face one another is the Street's public side. Children roller skate on the sidewalks and play kickball between passing cars. Women in housedresses, Big Boy's mother among them, watch from the stoops. She's a meaty woman with wobbly arms and flattened greasy hair who leans her elbows on the concrete balustrade, sole of one bare foot against the other knee. Proprietress of a ragged, unruly brood, she eyes the cars as if one might slow, bearing some prize she was promised and is still waiting for. Behind the row of houses is the private side, the alley where cars seldom come and men shambling from the Star-Brite stop for a first taste from bottles hidden in brown bags.

After sundown, as the heat slowly leaches from the sidewalks, Naomi, Mrs. Bledsoe, and Miss Odessa Adelaide sit on their porches overlooking the alley, fanning themselves and telling stories. Naomi and Miss Odessa sip iced tea from sweating glasses. Mrs. Bledsoe keeps a spare can of Ballantine in a bowl of ice on the floor beside her rocking chair. Their voices are low and intimate, sheltered by the night.

Upstairs on his porch, Neville strains to hear, *Tom Sawyer* open on his lap though it's too dark to read. The sheltering night pitches Miss Odessa's voice to the other women, secreting her words and leaving only the husk of her voice like the inside of her house that is dark and cool, smelling faintly of brown, flaking newspapers, clothes packed away in an attic.

Just as Mrs. Bledsoe is a widow, so too, in a way is Miss Odessa, though she calls herself Miss and her husband's still alive.

She'd thought she was happy, but he was a gambler, dedicated to dice, poker, horses, and the numbers. Saying she needed time, Miss Odessa left to go back to the house she'd married him to escape, the same house she lives in now. The truth was she already knew her own mind. When she came back, it was only for what she'd brought with her.

They were downstairs that last afternoon, her trunk and suitcases in the hall beside a box of framed photographs, when he said he wasn't going to try to change her mind because he wanted her to do what she thought best. But before she went—would she stay that night? Not forever, but just that night.

Before Miss Odessa can say what she'd done, what choice she'd made, Mrs. Bledsoe's rude cough splinters their intimacy.

"Oh, Odessa," she says, "Odessa, Odessa," and tilts the can, emptying it before she draws on her cigarette. When she flicks the butt into the darkness, it leaves a trail of glowing sparks. "You too old to keep concernin' yourself with that mess. Oughter be thankful you ain't got to fool with it no more."

"That might be true for you, 'Lina," Miss Odessa says, dignified, isolate, with the clear diction of the schoolteacher she became so as not to have to return home, "but it doesn't have to be for anybody else. And I'll tell you something. I'm not ashamed to admit it, but old as I am, not a night comes when I don't lay down in that bed and wish there was somebody beside me."

Mrs. Bledsoe lets out a strangled, "Huh!" that might be a cackle or a sob, before she reaches down for the last can of Ballantine.

"You're never too old," Miss Odessa says. "Not to want somebody. Isn't that right, Naomi?"

After a pause—is she pretending not to have heard, or does she want to ponder what she's been asked to settle?—Naomi says, "That's right, Miss Odessa. You're never too old," and Neville waits a long time in the silence that follows for Miss Odessa to finish her story. But she doesn't, and in a little while the women say good night and go in. Neville goes too, feeling cheated and disappointed, as if he'd paid for the movies and the film had broken in the projector just before the end. He needs to know, and not just because he wants to learn what happened.

Miss Odessa's story could have been one of the movies he sees previews for Saturdays at the Sylvan and that his mother sometimes treats him to when she gets home from the library and doesn't want to go to the pictures alone. But they're in color, and Miss Odessa's story happened so long ago it was another time entirely. So he sees it in black and white, like one of the old pictures he watches on the small, flickering television after school, drinking a glass of milk and eating a handful of cookies before his mother comes home to ask whether he's begun his homework. He doesn't always understand the people, why they say what they say and do what they do, doesn't always understand whether they deserve what happens to them. But he watches anyway, hoping to learn some secret that will help make sense of the new world he's come to.

and then it's August and the roses in Mrs. Bledsoe's garden have wilted from the heat and the petals fallen from the bushes. The branches of the peach tree are nubbled with fruit turning pale yellow and pink. Mrs. Bledsoe's prediction comes true—the heat and the humidity make everyone crazy. Sirens split the night on the Avenue, echoing the shouts and curses and, when they come out at all, the women go in early without telling stories.

Mrs. Bledsoe's upstairs boarder and his wife drive to the beach one morning, come back to sit on their porch late that evening with sand in their shoes and smelling of salt air. Mrs. Carver's a pert little woman in backless sundress, barefoot with red-painted toenails. Her husband, Mr. Carver, wears shorts and a straw hat tipped back on his head. He's a short, big-bellied man with rabbit-like front teeth and a thin mustache who works nights carrying special delivery mail. She's years younger. Mrs. Bledsoe and Miss Odessa speculate she married him for the money he surely must have saved being a bachelor so long.

They sit talking in low voices with an occasional chuckle, his voice with a whiskey huskiness, hers teasing. And then he says it's getting late; he's got to change and go see what they have for him to deliver down to the station. His wife says it's a shame they can't go out; why doesn't he just call in sick? He laughs a sweet whiskey laugh, says he wishes he could. She says he could if he wanted to, and he laughs some more and says it isn't his world, he just lives in it, and she says please, pretty please, almost like a little girl, and he says he has to go make him some money—what does she think pays the rent and keeps food in the refrigerator? And then she says, not quite teasing anymore, that he must not love her. She says it again, and he asks what she's talking about, says, I married you, didn't I, sweet whiskey laughter entirely gone. Married you so you didn't have to carry your behind back to Sleepy Hollow or Horse Pasture or Bump Ass or wherever it is you come from.

He goes inside then. In a little while she follows to fix his supper before he goes out to work.

The sun's setting and the alley streetlights flickering when she comes out again, changed into a bathrobe and pulling at a cigarette. Her face glistens moistly. She raises one hand to wipe it and the front of her robe opens, showing plump, round breasts, nipples dark as plums, the shadow at the cleft of her legs.

Naked in her grief for all the world to see, Mrs. Bledsoe's boarder's wife stands smoking, a lonely angel keeping vigil in the darkness.

wilson does not come on Saturday, but Neville goes out to the movies anyway, hoping he'll find him already there. If it were the two of them, they'd walk the long way because of Big Boy Bullock, turning left up the Street and then right at the corner by the apartments to go down to the Avenue. But it's Wilson Big Boy's after, not him, so Neville goes straight towards the Avenue because he doesn't want to miss the previews and the newsreel.

When he sees Wilson by the drugstore gum machines, he wishes he'd gone the long way. Big Boy's there, and P.J., Shepherd, and Chunk and two more whose names Neville doesn't know. Wilson's in the middle, biting his lip and trying not to look scared as Big Boy takes a crumpled paper from the front pocket of his jeans. It's Wilson's cartoon from the next-to-last day of school.

"Why you got to do me like this?" Big Boy demands. "Huh? Why you got to do me like this?"

Fisting trembling hands, Wilson jams them in his pockets. Now that it's almost over, he's resigned to whatever will happen, so he manages a laugh as if it doesn't matter. And besides, Big Boy should already know the answer.

"I'd known you was gon' keep it," he says, "I'da signed my name." He looks around the circle of boys. "Anybody got a ink pen or something I can write with?"

Big Boy laughs, a wolfish snarl, throwing back his head. "You got heart," he says. "I give you that. You shonuff got heart."

"Big Boy," Neville says, voice thin and weak, as if he were the one who's finally had the bad luck to find himself trapped by the gum machines. "What's happening?"

Big Boy glances at him dismissively before he goes back to the paper he's holding.

"Go on home," he says. "This ain't got nothin' to do with you."

It's permission to leave, to run home or continue on to the Sylvan, but Neville only looks up and down the Street, hoping for somebody who'll intervene. Inside the drugstore, a fat man in a sweat-stained hat heaves himself up from a stool at the lunch counter, idly working a toothpick between thick lips. He pauses a moment as if savoring the last of the air conditioning, and then opens the door to push through the boys clustered outside.

"Can't we talk about this?" Neville says.

For an instant, they're too stunned to speak. And then they're laughing and Neville can't believe he really did say it. He flushes hot, wishing again he'd come the other way.

"Talk 'bout what?" Big Boy says. "You his kin or sumpin'? You gon' take up for him?" He says, speaking slowly and patiently, as if some deficiency in Neville requires it. "That's awright with me. I don't care which onea y'all it is—somebody gon' give me some satisfaction."

Frozen by Big Boy's wolfish grin, Neville feels curiously, preternaturally aware, both inside and outside himself. He can see himself beside Wilson, see the men and women passing by unaware, a woman in overalls and thick-soled brogans under the Star-Brite awning, cigarette-hoarse voice haranguing two men.

"Naw, naw," she brays, voice carrying through the heat, "y'all got it all fucked up. This how that shit go."

Screwing up her scarred face beneath the red bandanna knotted at her forehead, she coughs as if suddenly self-conscious, puts hands behind her back as if it's a schoolroom recitation. And says:

Banker's daughter,
Down on her knees,
Cryin' "Shine, oh Shine,
Won't you save me please?"

Shine say, "Lookin' good,
And you shonuff fine,
But I surely must save,
My own ass this time."

The three loiterers erupt in coarse laughter, and Neville understands it's a sign, a gift that tells him he doesn't have to stay.

Because he doesn't want it to be him that has to give Big Boy satisfaction. Not that he doesn't want to help Wilson. But he isn't Wallace, Wilson's older brother who bests bigger boys because he fights as if his very sense of himself depends on not losing. He can't fight Big Boy, so who'd blame him if he decided to save himself this time?

Still, there's this that keeps him in the circle of sweating boys that sweltering August afternoon: Wilson's his friend, the one who helped make things easier after his mother announced they wouldn't be going back to Freeport because they were staying in her father's house. It was Wilson who showed him the shortcuts through the alleys behind the houses, showed him how to collect discarded soda bottles to trade for Red Hots and jawbreakers at the corner stores. Come winter, he's promised, when it snows they'll borrow shovels and make enough money clearing steps and sidewalks to go to the Lincoln on U Street or one of the gilded first-run movie palaces downtown.

Not knowing where the words or the idea come from, but hoping it will be enough, Neville says, "Lookahere, y'all—I know where there's some peaches."

he'd hoped they'd find Mrs. Bledsoe on her porch sipping ale as she smoked her Chesterfields, muttering imprecations like spells to protect her crop. But the rocking chair's empty and the kitchen light off, the back door closed behind steel security bars, so there's nothing for it but to follow Big Boy and everyone else over the fence.

The peaches are firm-soft, warm and ripe from the summer sun. They gorge themselves, lost in the sweetness, sucking the flesh from the pits once they're finished. But there is such abundance soon they're only taking a bite or two before throwing the rest to the ground to find another even more perfect. When they can eat no more, they begin to throw them—at one another, at the wall of Mrs. Bledsoe's house, outside the fence to see who can toss one the farthest up the alley.

And then Mrs. Bledsoe's at her kitchen window, roaring, "You little niggers better get the hell out my yard!"

She's at the door fumbling with the lock as they sprint towards the fence, pushing and shoving to be the first to gain it, the first over. Then they're spilling down the alley,

Wilson, P.J., Shepherd, and Chunk, everyone except Neville who's straddled on top the fence, toe of one tennis shoe in the chain link.

"Help me get the fuck off this," Big Boy says, flailing on tiptoe, snagged on a wire. "Help me."

Neville hesitates, looking towards the porch where Mrs. Bledsoe's opening the steel-barred security door. The other boys are disappearing through the mouth of the alley.

"C'mon, man," Big Boy says, pleading now, and for a moment Neville considers swinging his leg over and dropping back into Mrs. Bledsoe's yard to free him or at least share what will happen when Mrs. Bledsoe catches them.

And then he pushes himself over and falls, staggering before he rights himself on the cobblestones.

"Sorry," he says. "But Shine gotta save his own ass this time."

Mrs. Bledsoe's curses and Big Boy's pleading threats follow him down the alley.

blocks away on the corner where the Street meets the Avenue, they can't see Big Boy's mother, summoned by the telephone's shrilling, waddle fiercely down the sidewalk in crushed-heel slippers, can't witness her return, Big Boy's arm clamped firmly while she smacks the back of his head with her meaty hand, loudly promising once they're home she'll beat his sorry behind till he can't sit down. Chests heaving, hands and faces still sticky, they wonder at their narrow escape, challenge each other with claims about who was first over the fence, taunt Chunk about his singular lack of speed. And then the exhilaration fades and their laughter dies as they realize that already Mrs. Bledsoe must be on the telephone, calling each of their mothers and fathers.

"Aw, fuckit," Shepherd says at last. "Le's go to the show. Anybody got any money?"

the picture's just starting as they settle into their seats. First there are the girl groups, sleek and sexy in long, sequined form-fitting gowns—the Marvelettes, Martha and the Vandellas, the Supremes. Marvin Gaye's next, smooth and suave. And then, after Marvin's duet with Tammi Terrell, come Junior Walker and his All Stars, Rufus Thomas in purple shorts and knee-high white boots, Carla Thomas and Otis Redding, Smokey Robinson and the Miracles.

"And now, ladies and gentlemen," the M.C. on screen announces, "the man you've been waiting for, the Godfather of Soul, the Hardest Working Man in Show Business, the indefatigable, the incredible, never equaled and never excelled—James Brown," and the waves of excitement that've risen and crested with each new act reach a crescendo. Somehow, the band—horns, guitar, bass, and drums—cuts through the screams as James Brown bounds out onto the stage, spinning and stutter-stepping to the slick, syncopated beat.

Shepherd springs from his seat and dances into the aisle, dances down to gyrate in front of the screen. Shining his flashlight, the usher dances down to Shepherd, tucks the flashlight into his back pocket, beam still shining, grabs Shepherd by belt and collar. He dances him over to the emergency exit beside the screen and out the door.

On and on James Brown goes, beyond human endurance, glossy hair falling into his eyes, sweat beading his face. Cradling the microphone in one hand, he drops to his knees, sings pleading with eyes closed. Two attendants come out, drape a cloak over his shoulders and help him to his feet. They lead him off the stage.

Halfway there, James Brown throws off the cloak and breaks free, bounding back to the microphone. It happens again, and then a third time, the two men laying the cloak on his shoulders and leading him off stage as if frightened this time he's gone too far, finally given too much of himself. And each time James Brown breaks free and comes back as if summoned by what he cannot resist.

The third time, he shrugs out of the cape and makes as if to throw it into the audience. He does it again, does it once more. The girls in the Sylvan spring to their feet with stretched-out hands, as if some magic will send the cape flying from the screen. Faces solemn, his two keepers prise the cape from James Brown's fingers and lead him away.

This time, he does not come back. The band swings hard into his closing theme, pounding bass and syncopated drums, patent-leather horns.

Now Neville understands, and it doesn't matter that he still doesn't know what a bag is or why it's brand new. He's seen James Brown.

"i try me best," Ivan says, "look at it again and again from all sides, but I can't mek meself understand why you waste all that fruit 'stead eating it. I try, but I can't understand."

Neville stands with his head down, not daring to look at his father. The disappointment in his father's eyes hurts worse than if he'd taken off his belt and told him to stand gripping the back of a chair with his trousers down. His father's seldom struck him, even in Freeport, but he almost wishes he'd do it now.

"I 'owno," he says finally, just to say something so it will be over. "Just somethin' to do, I guess."

His mother winces.

"You don't have to talk like that," she says. "You're not like them."

But he does and he wants to be, even though he doesn't know how to say it. He remembers what it felt like sprinting up the alley and then coming back home after they'd sat through the movie a second time, everyone talking excitedly as they relived the show. It was the first time he felt he belonged, the first time he was no longer an outsider looking in. But he doesn't know how to tell her and so, in a little while, his father says if he wants to be stubborn, he can go to his room and just stay there.

Outside, dull thuds punctuate Mrs. Bledsoe's curses. Neville creeps to his porch and looks over the railing. She's attacking the tree with an ax. Piles of severed limbs lie around her on the concrete walk.

Night comes and the streetlights turn on and his mother opens the door, carrying a tray with a sandwich, an apple, and a glass of milk. Naomi sets the tray on the desk where he does his homework, stands looking at him with the same disappointment he'd seen on his father's face. Neville goes to lie down, turning to face the wall so he cannot see her.

"All you had to do was ask," Naomi says sadly. "I'm sure Mrs. Bledsoe would have given you more peaches than you could eat."

There's no answer he can make because he knows it's true. Naomi goes out, closing the door behind her. Mrs. Bledsoe's ax sounds against the tree, longer intervals between each blow, though her curses have not slowed.

She's killing something she loved, and now Neville understands what there's no one there to tell him, the point of Miss Odessa's story, the reason Mrs. Bledsoe's boarder's wife begged her husband to stay, why his father gave up everything to leave Freeport so he can rouse himself in the afternoons to go out to the Star-Brite. It's all for love, but as much as you need love to belong, to be part of something that you might live whole and entire or simply so as not to be alone, love seems as awful and terrifying as reaching into the fire to seize a hot coal.

Neville gets up from his bed, closes the window and the porch door against the heat, able no longer to bear witness to the core of pain in the torrent of Mrs. Bledsoe's abuse. Yet even with the door closed she continues to accuse him with mad, inchoate howls, like an animal abandoned by the master for whom it's given up its freedom.

AMONG THE RIGHTEOUS

A D.C. woman can be a hard-headed woman, and so Odis Renfro, newly released from his job as janitor, stock clerk, and general handyman at Speidell's Auto Parts Warehouse, pauses on the Avenue, two blocks from home, thinking of how best to tell his wife. Like Odis himself, the Avenue has seen better days. The fronts of the stores are faded, and the window of the laundromat on the corner is held together by a bolted square of plywood. Across the street, the barber Lamarr Jenkins stands in the window of his shop, one eye on the Avenue, the other on the head of the customer in his chair. He waves, but Odis does not see him.

Nearby, several men stand in the shade of Star-Brite Liquor, sharing a sullen useless fierceness. One, different from the others—he has only one good eye and, better-dressed, sports yellow, round-toed shoes with high heels—says, "I'ma tell y'all the truth." His other eye is milky-white, a dead pearl; he cocks his head, favoring his good eye, and for a moment Renfro thinks the one-eyed man is looking at him.

The one-eyed man says, "Ain't nothin' mess over a man worse than to let a bitch get hol' of his min'." The men's laughter comes, profane and emptily profound. Another, standing near the gutter, elbows on the square blue trash receptacle, says, "Preach it, Night Train. A bitch mess up yo' min' inna minit!"

And Renfro goes on, a tall, stoop-shouldered man in green khaki pants and a matching jacket with his first name, Odis, embroidered in red letters over the left pocket, still thinking of what Daisy will say.

9

at supper, odis Renfro finds his wife demanding he do something about the shoes their oldest son, Wallace, is wearing. The boy, almost thirteen, had bought them that same day with money earned from his paper route. The shoes have round toes and chunky high heels and are in fashion that spring among the jobless young and not-so-young men who line the Avenue from late morning until long after midnight. For that reason, Daisy Renfro thinks them unseemly for the son of a deacon at the One Faith United Baptist Church.

After seeing the shoes, Odis agrees, although they remind him—in spirit, if not shape—of a knob-toed, patent-leather pair with thin soles he himself had bought when it was still important no one know how recently he had come from the South.

"Well," he says slowly to the boy. "You got the receipt?"

Wallace nods sullenly, looking down at his plate and his half-eaten dinner. His brother, Wilson, five years younger, pushes his glasses up on his nose as he looks from his father to Wallace and back to his father again. The glasses, round and wire-rimmed, came from the clinic. They are always falling down. Both boys are cocoa brown, but Wallace is sharp featured with darting eyes that size up and appraise, while Wilson, his face still pudgy with baby fat, gazes about him serenely but intently, as if looking past the surface of things to some deeper meaning.

"Good," Odis says. "You ain't wore 'em that long. I guess you can take 'em back and get your money."

"Why?" Wallace says.

"Because," Odis replies, "I said so."

When Wallace says nothing, Odis motions for Daisy to pass him the bowl of greens. He dumps a spoonful on his plate, sets the bowl pointedly in front of Wallace—who has managed to get through the meal without taking any—and begins to eat again, nodding at Daisy as if the matter has been settled. Daisy purses her lips and looks doubtful.

"Why I gotta take 'em back?" Wallace says. He starts in a deep bass and ends in a high squeak; his voice is changing. He frowns, sticking out his lower lip as he looks defiantly at Odis. "I paid for 'em with my own money."

Odis chews without haste and swallows. He sets his fork down and rests his elbows on the table, looking over his folded hands at the boy. Daisy sighs from the other end of the table.

"Wallace, have some greens," she says. "And Wilson, eat your dinner. Times hard enough without you wastin' food in this house. Plenty of people be glad to have what you left lyin' there." The spoon clinks against the china as Wallace takes a small helping of greens and Daisy looks half warningly, half imploringly at Odis.

"Because they ain't no kinda shoes for a boy to be wearin'," Odis says with an exaggerated, fradulent patience that means he has heard enough. "You wanted to spend your money on shoes, you shoulda bought some like them school shoes your momma bought you in September."

Wallace sweeps his arm over the table in a gesture that dismisses sturdy oxfords and all sensible things. "Them ain't no kinda shoes," he says disdainfully, and Wilson giggles. "Them baby shoes. I want me some shoes like a man wear, not no schoolboy shoes."

"Well, what you think you is?" Odis levels his forefinger at the boy. "You gon' take back them shoes. First thing after school tomorrow. You gon' take back them shoes... Or my name ain't Odis Renfro."

"Uh uh," Wallace says under his breath.

"Whatchu say?" Odis thunders.

"Uh uh," the boy says. "I ain't gon' do it."

Odis stands, tearing the napkin from his neck in one swift motion. The boy starts, pushing back his chair so that it clatters to the floor. After a moment, he bends to pick it up. His eyes never leave his father's stony face. "Odis," Daisy pleads, but the two of them glare at each other—one defiant, the other overcome with anger at that defiance—each with the same high forehead and jutting, determined jaw. Wallace shakes his head once.

"Uh uh," he says again.

"Awright," Odis says. "We gon' see about that," and he yanks the boy upstairs, straps him several times with his own belt, and watches as he gets into bed.

Odis comes downstairs muttering that he is still the man in the house, he puts the meat on the table and the clothes on their backs and, by God, he is going to be respected. Daisy and Wilson finish the meal looking at their plates. It is the first time Odis has struck either of the boys.

shortly before five o'clock that Tuesday, Speidell, a bullnecked white man with a mush-mouth southern Virginia accent, had asked Odis to put the closed sign in the window of the Grand Prix Auto Parts Store and step back into the office. There, amid cartons stacked waist-high on the floor and belts of various sizes hanging from nails in the walls, Speidell removed a box of sparkplugs from his chair and sat down behind the desk.

Odis remained standing.

Speidell said that after almost seventeen years he knew Odis would understand. It wasn't that he didn't need him, and it wasn't that Odis wasn't a good worker. It was just that times, as Odis surely knew, were hard and, until they got better, he was just going to have to try to keep the store going by himself.

Odis almost dropped the cap he had been turning in his hands. All he could think to do was say he understood. Speidell, obviously relieved, took a folded-over check from his shirt pocket, gave it to Odis, and shook his hand.

When Odis looked while waiting for the bus, he noted that the check was for two weeks, three days more than he had worked. He buttoned it away in his shirt pocket, grudgingly grateful, but he knew that once the money was gone he would be unable to do the one thing a man should be able to do—support his family.

By the time he tells Daisy about it after they have gone upstairs to bed, Odis is mad. He is mad at Speidell for letting him go after seventeen years where he has hardly missed a day, mad at the conditions he does not fully understand that have made it necessary, and mad at himself because he knows he lost his temper with Wallace only because he had been laid off.

"Of course I know times is hard," Odis says fiercely, keeping his voice low so as not to wake the two boys asleep in the room across the hall. "That Speidell don't know nothin' 'bout hard. Let him come live this side of town like we do, he wanna learn somethin' 'bout it."

"Uh huh," Daisy says in vague assent, and turns to the window. The light from the street shines through a place where the curtains do not quite meet, showing the paper curlers twisted throughout her graying hair. A man and a woman pass underneath the open window, their footsteps and laughter echoing after they have gone. Two blocks away, on the Avenue, a siren slashes the air.

Odis stands and closes the window. He has light brown skin and graying hair that is cut close on the sides and thinning on top. Silhouetted against the window, he is as thin as he was in the gold-framed wedding picture on the dresser. People who do not know them well think he is younger than Daisy.

"That all he said?" she asks, patting the top of the bedside table, searching for her glasses. "He didn't say nothin' 'bout how long?"

"Naw." Odis sits heavily on the bed. "You know how he is. If I ast him, he say—"

The floor in the hall outside their bedroom creaks and Daisy raises herself from where the mattress sags towards the center and turns on the light. She has wide shoulders and heavy arms under her nightgown. "Wilson?" she calls. "Which onea you boys is that?"

"Wallace, ma'am," he squeaks.

"What you doin' up? Tomorrow's a school day."

"I ain't up," Wallace says gruffly. "I just had to get me a drink of water."

"Boy," Odis says, starting to rise, "don't you sass your—" but Daisy has her hand on his shoulder.

"Well, get it then," she says. "And get right to bed. You hear?" She turns to plump her pillow and then settles back against it, not waiting for the boy's response.

Odis says, "You know if I was to ast him, all Speidell say is he can't say."

Daisy sighs. "I worry about that boy," she says. "You was too rough on him tonight."

"Ain't nothin' wrong with him, 'cept his head still hard. But I guess you right—I ain't had to do all that to let him know just 'cause he wear long pants and buy his own shoes don't make him a man."

Daisy looks at him over her glasses and Odis looks away. He shifts, starts to get up, and then lies down again. It is on her face that they have been putting it off and can afford to do so no longer.

"You know we can't make it on what we got saved," Daisy says. "Not for long."

Odis passes his hand over his jaw, making a small scratching sound on the stubble. He shifts uneasily on the bed so that he and Daisy slide closer to each other.

"I know it," he says softly. "Didn't figure it exactly, but I knew it. But what else am I gon' do, 'cept go out and look for another job? Times is hard, just like the man said."

"You could go back and tell the man he cain't fire you," Daisy says.

Odis swings his head to look at her. Her tone was so deliberate and the answer so quick that he knows she must have come on it while listening when he told her what Speidell had said before giving him the check. Daisy looks back at him, brown eyes calm and unwavering, and Odis turns away, asking himself what in the world he has done to deserve such a hard-headed woman.

"Speidell just did what he had to do," he says mildly, hoping to persuade her before she latches too firmly onto the idea. "Business been bad all last year. It ain't his fault."

"Didn't say it was," Daisy says. "But as long as you worked for that man, he owe you more than, 'Sorry Odis, but I got to let you go.' You got a wife and two children to feed. You got house payments to make and bills to pay. Just like he do. Go tell him that."

While he wonders what to say to her, Odis thinks of the patent-leather shoes he once owned. He was not yet married then, and he had been working for Speidell for about six months. He was never without money. There were mornings he came to work having slept only two or three hours, the taste of gin still in his mouth. He had worn the shoes to dancehall and poolroom until the leather veneer began to split, showing the cheap cardboard beneath. He had never bought another pair like them; shortly afterwards, he met

Daisy and realized—it was one of her first questions—that he had not been to church since leaving home.

"I can't do that," Odis says. "Every day for the past seventeen years I gone in there and work' for that man. He can't treat me no better, I'll get me another job. Might even take my time, till I find what I want. I could use a few days' rest."

He can feel her disbelief, as solid and as real as her body beside him. The truth is, Speidell does owe him more than a handshake and three days' extra pay. But he cannot do what she is saying. The galling humiliation of such an appeal is not all that prevents Renfro from denying it possibilities. More simply, he cannot imagine himself confronting Speidell with the proper impassiveness that will make his return inevitable. This he does not tell Daisy.

"Awright." Daisy sets her glasses on the table and flicks off the light. "But bills not gon' stop comin' just 'cause you restin'," she says, turning and settling to give Odis the broad expanse of her back. "What you gon' do then?"

"I don't know, woman," Odis says. "But right now, I'm gon' try and get me some sleep."

there are, besides those who must eat in the Renfro household, payments on the house itself and other bills that arrive with the impersonal regularity of first and fifteenth. These are the things a man must see to. For the next several mornings, Renfro rises early to ride the bus, clutching folded-over pages from the want ads with whole columns circled.

After watching him return mute in the afternoons with a pocketful of useless, hoarded transfers, Daisy can no longer refrain.

"You fin' anything?" she asks.

Odis shakes his head. "Not yet. But it's only a matter of time before I get lucky."

By now, of course, the boys know, and so Daisy determines to wait.

"You know," she says brightly, "I saw 'Lina Bledsoe this afternoon. She stop' me on the street and tell me she hit the number. Just had to tell all she was gon' do with that money."

"That right," Odis says.

"She say she win three hundred dollars. Played seven-six-one."

Odis, looking at Wallace, says, "Boy, you take back them shoes?"

"Uh huh," Wallace says.

"Whatchu mean 'uh huh?' Yes or no?"

"Odis," Daisy says, and Wilson says, "He took 'em back, Poppa."

"Awright." Odis says, to Daisy, "Well, Miz Bledsoe sure is lucky."

"That's right." Daisy stands to clear the table. "But luck comes and it goes. You can't count on it to take care of you all the time."

they sit downstairs after the boys have gone to bed. Daisy sews a patch on a pair of Wilson's jeans. Odis looks at the newspaper, searching the narrow columns in the back of the sports pages.

Finally, Daisy turns the pants to the light and draws the needle through. "You go to Speidell?" she says.

"Naw." Odis raises the paper to hide his face even more. "What kind of man am I gon' look like, go beggin' Speidell for my job?"

Daisy knots the thread and raises it to her mouth to bite off the end. Sticking the needle into the pincushion on the table beside her, she turns the pants to the next hole and adjusts the patch. She fixes it with pins and takes up the needle again.

" 'A haughty spirit go before a fall,' " she says at last. "Least, that's what the Book say. Or did you forget?"

When Odis makes no response, Daisy sets down her sewing.

"Why you have to be so stubborn, Odis? It ain't for me I want you to go back there. You see me runnin' around wearin' jewelry and fancy clothes, goin' to the beauty shop every weekend? We ain't even got a car. But I want us to own this house for the boys, and I want to put somethin' away for them, so they can go further in this life than we did. Go talk to the man, Odis."

"Lemme tell you somethin'," Odis says, putting down the paper. His voice is trembling. "My daddy thought you had to be that way. He'd step off a sidewalk and grin, 'cause that's what you had to do just to get by. Me, soon as I was old enough, I caught the first thing smokin' and come up here. Speidell don't want me, I'll go where somebody else do. I learned a long time ago that you can't always win. But least you can go where you don't have to fight."

Daisy squints at her sewing and stabs the cloth with her needle. Odis turns the page, making the newspaper crackle.

"I wouldn't know anything about that," she says.

"You never had to, not livin' up here."

In a little while Daisy sets down the sewing and takes off her glasses.

"I'm goin' to bed," she says. And when Odis does not move, "You comin', Mr. Renfro?"

Odis folds the paper and sets it down.

"Yeah," he says wearily. "I'm comin'."

ⵔ

on the afternoon of another gray day of worry, Odis Renfro eats with a slow abstractedness that precludes enjoyment, pours himself a second cup of coffee, listening as he sips it to the vigorous thumps of Daisy upstairs.

These days he no longer goes out. They have become akin to Saturdays, but empty, without mornings for him to take hammer and saw and, with sure brown hands, set about the tasks she has saved for him. In the end, there is the rich evidence of a thing set right and well-made. And afterwards, the slow walk to the church, floors to wax and polish, pews to dust in the still holiness of the sanctuary. And then the fine solace of the barbershop and the balm of Lamarr Jenkins's hands, laughter and cigar smoke and the nimble swapping of lies, small sips in the back room from a bottle covered by a brown paper bag. And finally, home, dinner, and sometimes—more rarely now—the sweetness of coaxing Daisy's body from the cocoon of its stolidity, a mutal easing with shy wonder and circumspection; the boys sleep in the room across the hall.

Odis goes to the landing and calls: "C'mon down and have some coffee wid' me, sugar. Pot still warm."

Another thump and Daisy comes, balancing a wicker basket against one hip, says, passing without stopping so that he must yield the way: "Four people's dirty clothes and sheets to wash and iron and I'm late gittin' started. I ain't got time to siddown." She looks at him pointedly. " 'Less you gon' help with the laundry."

It is then that Odis Renfro decides to go out to the barbershop.

ⵔ

lamarr jenkins looks up from dusting rows of multicolored lotions, oils, and ointments, trying to hide his surprise when Renfro walks in. Renfro tosses his cap on the hatrack. He sits and says, with a heartiness he does not feel, "Afternoon, Mr. Jenkins. Guess I'll take my usual today." The two men are alone in the shop.

Jenkins gives the bottles one last flick before he sets down the duster and adjusts his green eyeshade. He lowers the chair, winds the tissue paper around Odis's neck, sweeps a clean striped cloth over his knees, draws it up under his chin. Pinning it, he pats him once on the shoulder and turns to select clippers. Odis, looking out the window, can see the men on the corner. And then Jenkins begins, and he closes his eyes under the soft, soothing hum.

"You in kinda early," Jenkins says. "Take off from work?"

"More like it took off from me. Los' my job."

Jenkins stops, holding the clippers away from Odis's neck.

"You kiddin' me, man. Down at the auto parts store?"

"Thass right."

"Man." Jenkins shakes his head and lowers the clippers again. "After all them years, thass a hell of a note. What you gon' do now, Deacon?"

Odis thinks about the day Speidell called him into the back room.

"Keep lookin'," he says. "Just like I been doin'."

Jenkins considers this. Once, there were two other barbers, the three chairs filled and a long-headed boy or a woman with slick hair waiting, but now, with the passing of each first of the month, Jenkins, uncomplaining, has time to look out at the Avenue. He turns the chair for better perspective on the thinning hair over which Odis has granted him custody. He says, "You fin' something, Deacon. Jus' a matter of time."

Odis says nothing. The barbershop smells of bay rum and powder, and the hum of the clippers is as comforting as rain on a tin roof. He could go to sleep in the peace of the enameled steel chair's cracked leather.

"Daisy awright?"

"Takin' it bad. I just wish somebody hadda tol' me when I come up here that a DeeCee woman is a hard-headed woman."

Jenkins chuckles, and Odis says, "Tell the truth, it's my boy I'm worried about. Wallace come home the other night with some shoes."

"Shoes? What kinda shoes?"

"I don't know whatchu call 'em. Got round toes and high heels. Bottoms look like they an inch thick. Say he don't want no schoolboy shoes. Then he sass me at the dinner table—his momma sittin' right there. I took him upstairs and showed him whose house he livin' in."

Jenkins laughs softly under his breath. Odis laughs too, and Jenkins says, without reproach, "You too hard on that boy, Odis. How old he now? Fifteen? Sixteen?"

"Shoot, he ain't but workin' on thirteen. But I guess you right—I ain't had to do all that to let him know just 'cause he wear long pants and think he got somethin' to put in 'em, that don't make him a man."

In the silence that follows, Odis thinks of the shoes he himself once owned. More than once, he had shambled to his rented room drunk in them. Until the leather veneer had torn and the repairman to whom he'd taken them had said they were not worth repairing, his tone making it clear Odis had been a fool. It was shortly after that he met Daisy and, without undue struggle, surrendered.

Jenkins finishes, shutting off the clippers for the last time, prepares the towel dusted with talcum powder. Odis, reluctant to leave the security of the chair for the new-found hazards of home, asks for a shave. "Thass extra," Jenkins says automatically, and Odis nods; both men have known for a long time.

The barber is lathering his face, looking from time to time out the window, when he stops.

"Deacon," he says, and in his voice there is that he does not believe what he is seeing. "Look out the window. Ain't that your boy?"

When Odis sits up, he sees Wallace, wearing the new shoes he has been told to return, taking out cigarettes and handing them around to the men on the corner. Wilson stands nearby. Halfway to the door, Odis remembers the cloth around his neck. He tears it off, scattering the safety pin to the floor. Jenkins comes out after him, holding the shaving brush.

"Boy, whatchu doin' out here?" Odis growls, and Wallace puts the cigarettes behind his back. He looks at Odis defiantly, and from between sullen lips comes the word, "Nothin'."

The one-eyed man smiles, stroking his chin with a furtive slyness as he regards Odis's mad-dog face. His companions smile too, but Odis is looking at his boys. Wilson shifts from foot to foot, as if he has to go to the bathroom and is waiting for someone to give him permission.

"Poppa?" Wilson says, pulling at his arm. Odis bends to listen. "Wallace jus' tryin' to git his money. He been givin' Night Train his lunch money to play the number for him."

Odis looks wonderingly at Jenkins over the boy's head. Jenkins looks as if he wants to laugh, and Odis stands.

"That right?" he says mildly.

Wallace nods. "Played seven-six-one," he says. "Jus' like Miz Bledsoe. Won me almost a hundred dollars." And then, "Somebody got to be the man in the house and bring home some money."

Jenkins, still trying not to laugh, says, "You give your money to this man? This man here?"

Wallace says, "Night Train, that's his name."

Now the laughter that has been bubbling inside Jenkins explodes, and the barber with the wet brush soaking the pocket of his smock, throws back his head, and laughs. Odis permits himself a thin smile.

"Night Train?" Jenkins chokes out. "He call hisself that now? When he first come up here from Arkansaw—an' had enough money to come in my shop—somebody give him that name. Say he look like he only got one headlight—"

"—An' make so much noise you can hear him comin' in the dark," Odis finishes, and the two men laugh, deep, full, rich laughter, the laughter that still comes Saturday night in the barbershop, when they remember that once they were young and the nights endless, and it was nothing to wake up with the taste of gin in their mouths and go out again, because it was the thing to do, to earn their bread.

"Man...," Night Train starts, and Wallace looks down at his new shoes. Wilson looks once at Night Train, and then he nods to himself.

These, Odis thinks, are his boys, both his boys that are so different. All at once he knows that if God granted him one wish, it would not be for himself or for Daisy, but that each of his sons could exchange what was lacking in him for what the other had in abundance, that Wallace's mindless enthusiasm might be tempered with Wilson's caution, that Wilson would become more bold. And because this cannot be so, he knows there is only a little while for his love to protect them.

He says, to Night Train, "When I was a young man, I took care of myself with my fists and my feet. But I'm too old to fight now, and too proud to run. So I carry a friend in my pocket, and what I keep says you gon' give my boy back his money."

Now the other men drift away, as if heeding a call only they can hear. Night Train studies Odis's face. After a long moment, he says, "Cain't argue with that," and pulls out three crumpled dollar bills. He starts to hand them to Odis, but Odis says, "No," and Night Train gives them to Wallace.

The boys turn, ready to go, but Odis is not quite finished.

"Now," he says. "Numbers man, huh?" He looks at each of the boys. "Lemme tell you somethin'. You don't have to go lookin' for a numbers man, a real numbers man. A real numbers man come lookin' for you. 'Cause all he got is his word, and it's bad for business if people start sayin' you can't pay off."

Finished, he looks at Wallace. "Come here," he says gently.

And when the boy comes, he puts his arm around his shoulders, pointing at Night Train's retreating figure. He says, softly, so only Wallace can hear, "You think thass all there is to bein' a man?" and when the boy does not answer, swats him twice across the seat of the pants. The tears spring hotly to Wallace's eyes, but Odis ignores them.

"Go on," he says. "Tell yo momma I be home soon." And to Wilson, who stands looking up at his father, "You too. And don't let me catch y'all out here again."

later, standing behind the chair, Jenkins says, with the deference due a man he has seen with a woman not his wife, “Deacon, I didn’t know you carried a piece,” and Odis reaches under the cloth to take out key ring and coins, and a penknife no bigger than his thumb.

“Huh,” Jenkins says. And then, “He be awright. You got a good boy there. ’N’ you raisin’ him right. Gon’ grow up to make you proud.”

“Yeah,” Odis says. “If I don’t wear out his behind first.”

that evening, lying on the couch reading the newspaper, Deacon Odis Renfro looks up often, chuckling softly to himself, once even raising his hand and wiping his eyes. Daisy, turns her sewing and looks over at him with familiar suspicious tolerance. She frowns.

“Well,” Odis says after a while. “Guess I get up early in the morning and go talk to Speidell.”

“Good.” Daisy sticks the needle in the pincushion, searches in the pool of mending in her lap for some item small enough to complete before bedtime. “I knew you’d do right.”

“How you know?” Odis says.

“’Cause,” Daisy says. “I wouldn’t never of married you—let alone stayed this many years—if I didn’t know you could see it when you wrong.”

SEASONS

The tragedy of life is not that man loses,
but that he almost wins.

heywood broun

But in a last word to the wise of these days let it be said that of all who give gifts these two were the wisest. Of all who give and receive gifts, such as they are the wisest.

o. henry, "the gift of the magi"

Waiting for Garnet in the old Chevrolet, the radio on in the drowsy summer heat, the steady, cheerful voice of the announcer calling the game over the low murmur floating from the stands like paper caught in the wind, Tyson could almost imagine it was that game, the one he had told the boy about. He flexed one still-brawny arm cautiously, waiting for the twinge near his right elbow that was a reminder of that day.

His fingers curled, hand gripping an imaginary ball that was ready to streak toward Spider Collins's glove as if it had a life of its own. Tyson flexed his arm again, broad nostrils flaring as he exhaled. His eyes narrowed against the glare and he could see the Babe in the batter's box, pugnacious stance daring him to throw it. He pushed back his cap, nodded slowly, the tension mounting while he waited for the perfect moment...

And then Garnet wrenched open the door to the Chevy.

"Tyson Odom," she said, a little out of breath from the walk up the slope of the driveway. Tyson sat up straight, the little smile at the memory of the Babe's futile swing disappearing, clean-shaven face clouding with resignation. "Where have you been all this time with Jesse and Mrs. Wilcox's car?"

Garnet sat down, setting her handbag between them on the stained stuffing that poked through the split plastic seam. She was a stout woman with smooth, honey-gold skin and bright knowing eyes. "You've had her car for more than two hours. And if that wasn't enough, you had to go filling that child's head with all that baseball nonsense again."

Tyson shifted on the seat as he turned the key. She spoke better than he did; was as she never tired of reminding him, the daughter of the Reverend Mordecai Compton, founding pastor of Providence Congregational Church; had gone to Dunbar when it was still Dunbar, and then to Howard, if only for a little while—and he had been the reason for that.

The Chevy's engine rumbled and died, and Tyson turned the key again, stepping hard on the gas. The engine coughed, stuttered, and caught. He floored it twice before putting the Chevy in gear and releasing the balky clutch. The rusted, dented car bucked and clattered, an affront to the dignity of the quiet, tree-lined Chevy Chase street.

Tyson stole a glance at Garnet. She was looking directly at him, arms folded across her chest, waiting, he knew, for an answer.

"Took the car to have it washed," he said, choosing the easiest way by ignoring what she had said about the boy. "She asked me to."

"You could have done it yourself. You could have gotten the hose and washed it right there in the driveway."

"You know how much she offer' me?" Tyson was unable to keep his voice from rising. He turned the corner, heading for the avenue that would take them through Rock Creek Park and back into their part of the city. "One dollar. Shee-it. I wouldn't spit on a car for a dollar."

A smile crept stealthily across Garnet's face. "Hmmph," she said, and she tossed her head. Something about the movement of her still-slender neck made Tyson remember another time she had done it that same way. It was a long time before, but before he could think of when and where and what it had meant, Garnet passed her hand over her mouth, trapping the smile before it went too far.

"And had the boy with you all that time, telling him all those old stories. That's the first thing Jesse said when he came into the kitchen to get his sandwich and his glass of milk—'Tyson's been telling me about how he struck out Babe Ruth.' I said, 'Uh huh?' That's all I said."

The Chevy was up to thirty on the road that led to Rock Creek Parkway now, and Tyson turned up the radio so he could hear over the rattles and squeaks. He sat a little hunched forward, left elbow hanging out the window, right hand on the steering wheel. Beside him, Garnet took out a handkerchief from her handbag. It was hot in the car despite the breeze from the window.

"That's all I said," she said again, mopping the sweat freckled along her hairline. "'Uh huh? That's all I said." She wiped her forehead again and turned to him. "Tyson, why don't you tell that boy the truth about what happened?"

"Told him the way I remember it," Tyson growled, and Garnet said, "Between you and the two of them, no wonder that boy is the way he is.

"All your stories got him thinking he'll be a ballplayer. Always carrying around that glove—I bet he sleeps with it. Mrs. Wilcox made her husband send him away from the table yesterday evening because he wanted to eat with his glove on. I could hear him crying, all the way down in the kitchen. This morning, Mrs. Wilcox said when she went up to put him in bed, she found him packing his little bag. Said he was running away."

Tyson smiled, turning his head, but Garnet saw it.

"What are you grinning at? That boy's in real trouble if you and his parents are all he has to look up to."

"Now, that's not true," Tyson began, and Garnet said, "You think so?" She said, "What'd you do about the car?"

"Took it to the car wash. Whatchu think?"

"Three dollars. Well, at least she paid for it." Garnet turned to him, eyes narrowed. "She did pay for it?"

Tyson snorted and shook his head. "Woman, I told you. I wouldn't spit on a car for a dollar."

Tight-lipped, Garnet shook her head in resignation, folding her hands in her lap as she looked outside.

"Now just let me make sure I understand," she said, fury in her voice barely controlled, "Mrs. Wilcox offered you a dollar to wash her car, but you were too proud to do it yourself so you paid three dollars to take it to the car wash. And when you brought it back, you didn't ask her for the money?"

This was too much for him.

"You worried about that three dollars? Is that what you all het up about?" Steadying the wheel with one hand, Tyson unbuttoned his shirt pocket. "You always so worried 'bout money. Take a look at this." Garnet's eyes widened, and Tyson said, "Hit the number, sugar—three hundred and twenty-six dollars. Let's you and me go out tonight."

"Three hundred dollars?" Garnet's voice was wary. "You hit the number for that much?"

Tyson put the roll back in his pocket and patted the bulge.

"Three hundred and twenty-six dollars. Just now picked it up."

He looked over expansively, in time to see Garnet's eyes narrow again and her smile disappear. She reached and switched off the radio. Tyson looked back at the road, feeling as if he had glimpsed a familiar face in a crowded station and it had turned out to be a stranger's after all.

"Where'd you go to get it?"

"Barbershop. Where else you gon' find Sweet Man on a Saturday?"

"And you had Jesse with you," Garnet cried, "down there on the Avenue with all those low-life, no-good hustlers? You had Jesse down on the Avenue?"

"Hustlers? What hustlers? You call Jenkins on his feet all day with them clippers a hustler? And Sweet Man—cain't nobody say he ever missed no payout. Besides, woman, the boy was with me."

"Oh Lord." Garnet dabbed at her forehead with the handkerchief, unfolded it, and twisted it in her hands. "Tyson, you still don't see. What if Jesse tells his mother?"

"Shee-it." Tyson stepped on the pedal. The Chevy surged reluctantly. "That whatchu all worried about? The boy ain't gon' tell his momma. An' what if he did? Worse she could do is show you the door. The back door. You don't need to be doin' maid's work for them white folks noways. Coulda quit a long time ago—house well-nigh paid for, we got money in the bank, and it's just the two of us. But I guess you just loves them ol' white folks too much to quit."

As soon as he heard himself say them, Tyson wished he could take back the words. The Chevy's engine knocked mightily, protesting the unaccustomed strain, and he frowned, glancing at Garnet purse-lipped beside him. He eased off the gas, patting the steering wheel as if to soothe the ancient sedan. It wasn't the white folks; it was Jesse. And if Garnet did not understand what it was about himself and the boy, then that was all right—he himself did not know what the two of them talked about in the kitchen when the boy came home from school and his father was at the office and his mother at one of her clubs. But Tyson knew the truth, as Garnet must also: Without Jesse all they had left was each other.

"Housekeeper," Garnet said. "Housekeeper. That's what I am." Her voice was dull, as if the words were only ritual, and she looked off into the distance toward Georgia Avenue, as if she were somewhere else or wished she could be. "There's nothing wrong with keeping house for somebody else. And you know I like to have means of my own.

You never know what'll happen in this world—you of all people ought to have learned that much by now."

"I know, sugar," Tyson said, "ain't nothin' wrong with what you do. Nothin' at all," but Garnet was holding out her hand.

"Better let me keep that money," she said, "till I can get down to the bank on Monday."

Tyson sighed. "Sugar," he said, "sugar." Still Garnet held out the unsatisfied hand, honey-gold and work-worn from years of washing dishes, scrubbing floors, caring for other women's babies. Tyson sighed again and gave her the wad of bills.

It was easier to keep the peace.

after dinner, garnet sat on the plastic-covered sofa with her Bible, watching Tyson over the top of her glasses and smiling slyly to herself. He was crouched over the television, tilting the antenna and then stepping back to look at the screen before he twisted the antenna again. The Orioles were playing a twi-night doubleheader, and sometimes—if it was positioned just right—he could pick up the Baltimore station. But tonight, no matter how much he coaxed the set, the men on the field remained flickering ghosts, refusing to materialize out of the flutter and snow. Tyson swore softly and Garnet's sly smile broadened. Eventually, he would give up. It would take a while, but she could wait. For then there would be quiet in the house, and soon it would be time to sleep. In the morning she would go to church. She did not have to return to the Wilcoxes' till Monday.

Garnet squeezed her eyes shut against the tears that came with the realization this was all she had to look forward to. How in the world did I get to this place? she wondered.

The thought was so powerful she opened her eyes to look at Tyson, sure she must have spoken aloud. But no, he was still hunched over the television, still muttering softly to himself as he tried the antenna.

She sighed and gazed down at the open pages of her Bible, trying to find some comfort, some solace, some answer to her question. But it was no use; peace of mind required acceptance and acceptance forgiveness, and she could never forgive Tyson. Not for the years gone by so fast she knew now that it was too late; there would only ever be two parts to her life—the time before when it was still possible to dream, and afterwards, when it seemed that time had been only a dream, a dream that belonged to someone else.

Just beyond Tyson, on the piano beside the fireplace with its artificial logs, was a row of photographs—Garnet's parents; herself and her two sisters, Dorcas and Oralia, taken when Dorcas was a senior at Howard, Garnet a freshman, and Oralia still at Dunbar. The Rev. Compton had written "The Three Graces" on the bottom edge of the gray mat board in his elegant calligraphy. At the center, the place of honor, sat the picture of Garnet and their son, Warren, on the day of his graduation from medical school. Of the two in the picture, it was hard to tell who was proudest, mother or son. For Garnet it was the fulfillment of something she knew she herself no longer entitled to, but it was Warren's triumph. He smiled and held her hand, something hard and aloof in his eyes as he looked at Tyson behind the camera.

Grumbling softly to himself, Tyson gave up and sat down in his old chair, staring balefully at the blank screen. The windows in the living and dining rooms and the front and back doors were open, but it was hot inside the house. Only a slight breeze stirred the curtains. Tyson had taken off his khaki shirt. He sat now in a plain white sleeveless undershirt.

And who could blame Warren for wanting to leave his old life behind?, Garnet thought; if she'd allowed it, Tyson would have taken off the undershirt too.

Oh, but he was a stubborn man! The chair he sat in was stained and faded, the stuffing clumped into hard clots, the springs broken. It was the last piece of the old furniture in the house, the only one she had not had covered. She'd seen a commercial on television and called to have the new sofas and chairs covered in plastic, given the men two dollars to carry Tyson's old recliner out to the alley once they'd finished. When Tyson had come home that evening, he'd balked at the plastic slip covers. They stuck to his arms when it was hot, he complained, refused to warm to his body when it was cold. When a man sat down, he'd argued, he wanted good, honest cloth against his skin. Garnet had said the plastic was easier to clean. And that would have been that. Except that Tyson had salvaged his old chair before the trashmen could make it disappear, and so that was another thing to hold against him; except for the chair, the living room was just the way she wanted it.

"You could see if there's something else on," Garnet said sweetly. "A movie or some show."

He said nothing, but she could feel resentment emanating from him like the shimmering waves of heat from the street outside. Garnet smiled to herself; Tyson rarely watched anything but baseball, and it gave her some small satisfaction to share the disappointment in which her life was steeped. You wanted me, she thought. Yes you did. And now you have me.

"Naw," Tyson said wearily. "Don't feel like it." Without getting up from his chair, he reached towards the magazines on the coffee table. There were two neat fans, arranged to show the titles. He pawed through the closest and plucked out a copy of *Ebony*. The rest spilled over towards the center of the table. One fell to the floor. Garnet bent to get it and then pressed her back firmly against the sofa.

Outside, it was beginning to grow dark. Up the street the children called, playing One-two-three, Red Light! in the church yard, their cries mingling with the raucous chatter of sparrows.

When they'd moved onto the Street after the war, there had still been squirrels. There were white families on the block as well, and Tyson had unloaded the truck set-faced and stiffly polite, speaking when spoken to, ready to face whatever came. The white people were gone now, and so were the squirrels. And though they still knew most of their neighbors, if not to invite into their homes then by sight to wave to, the block had changed in other ways. The doctors and lawyers and schoolteachers had moved farther north or west towards the Park. There were still people like themselves, taxi drivers and government clerks and mail carriers, hard-working men and women who kept up their homes and saved to send their children to D.C. Teachers, Fisk, and Hampton. But there were more women without men and with too many children, and here and there, like a mouth with rotting teeth, the Street was dotted with houses with cracked concrete stoops and peeling paint.

Something moved across the living room, catching Garnet's eye, and she looked up from her Bible, still lost in her thoughts. It was Tyson. Slumped in his chair, covered with a sheen of sweat, he fanned himself with the magazine. The sight of him, common and crude in the white undershirt, made Garnet want to go up to the bedroom. But it was still too hot to consider the possibility of sleep. In an hour or two she would go up to shower.

It had been different when she was a girl; everything had been different. Men and women wore hats, people said hello on the street and, even if they were strangers, excuse me when they bumped into one another. Summers had been cooler. But perhaps it had been only the house in LeDroit Park with its great brass-trimmed, wood-paddled fans turning beneath high ceilings, the long white porch shaded and surrounded by trees.

The heavy sadness, as familiar as the bitter burden of resentment that galled her chest and throat, made Garnet blink back tears. How in the world did I get to this place? she thought again. How do any of us end up here? And suddenly she was afraid, afraid of the years remaining with so little to look forward to. She saw reflected in Tyson's slackening middle and thinning, graying hair signs of her own losing struggle with time, but there was no satisfaction in knowing love had whispered its lies and he, too, had listened, no satisfaction in knowing that time's truth had caught him out. Instead, Garnet mourned for Tyson as he had been, young and easy and careless of his strength, that first time when she had known she wanted him and would have him no matter what it cost. And knew now that in totting up her accounts of spite and grievances she had seen only part of the inevitable sum. You wanted me, and now you have me. But the rest of it was, just like I have got you.

And so they sat in silence, two old enemies abandoned together on an island. The darkness gathered outside and the children's cries faded as they straggled indoors. The birds subsided into stillness, broken only by the cars that slowed for the stop sign at the end of the block before moving on. Slowly the heat released its hold on the day. In a little while, Garnet closed her Bible.

"Well," she said. "I'm going upstairs."

After a moment, Tyson said, "Go on. I'll be up in a minute."

garnet snored softly with her mouth slightly open, lost in the sleep of the just, the sleep of the untroubled, the sleep of those who have made peace with the past. Her hair was done up in curlers, the thin sheet pulled up to her neck. The fan in the window thrummed softly. Beside her, Tyson sweated and swore to himself as he looked over at the lighted dial of the alarm clock.

It was after eleven, and he wanted to be outside, just getting started where there were crowds, soft lights, and a saxophone moaning over a piano's spilled notes. He wanted to dance an elegy for the long-gone careless ease with which he had once thrown and caught the ball; wanted to laugh and drink and fool himself into believing that tomorrow would be better because yesterday was just a bad dream. And afterwards go to Ben's for a big helping of chili, with someone who would crumble the crackers on top for him as they talked and ate, watching the fancy men and the hustlers, and the just plain folks like themselves out for a good time Saturday night.

He wanted a woman to do that with, and he wondered what in the world he had been thinking when he had told Jenkins this was what he and Garnet planned to do with Sweet Man's money.

Tyson closed his eyes, trying again to sleep, and saw instead Jesse's face, heard the boy ask him to tell him one more time about how he had struck out Babe Ruth. The body lied and betrayed, but the mind remembered; he didn't need to tell the story to know exactly how it had felt. Young and strong-armed, he had thought his shoulders would never stoop, his belly never thicken. Back then, the way he had been—and the way a part of him still believed he would always be—he could whip the ball down to the plate as if it were following a wire, make it curve wide, then slip back past an unsuspecting batter as if it was listening to his whisper to help it find its way.

He had used to be able to stay out all night, sleep on the bus on the way to the ballpark, then pitch nine good innings. And be ready to go again that evening or the next day—on the mound or in the outfield, just so long as he was playing ball. Reacting to the crack of bat on ball without thinking—knowing from the sound whether to bear down on himself the next time (because that ball was gone), or moving already (because it made a different sound, a sound that told him the man was as good as out), moving to the left or to the right, reaching up or stooping and scooping the ball into his glove (Damnit! Knowing it was there already!), whipping it over but hesitating first, a little hop, a skip, that said to the runner—"Here, I'll give you a step. And still get you out by two."

Garnet stirred and Tyson held himself still, waiting until her breathing became regular again. Pushing the sheet aside, he stepped out of bed. He stood for a moment in the breeze from the fan in the window, one hand stuck down the waistband of his pajama pants. The cool air was good on his bare chest. Finding his slippers with his feet, he wedged his toes into them and reached for his bathrobe.

Softly, so as not to wake her, Tyson padded downstairs, shuffling a little in the worn slippers. He walked softly through the dark living room to the kitchen, opened the door that led to the basement, and turned on the light. He stooped, reaching behind the shelf of cleanser and detergent for the fifth of Seagram's.

Garnet knew that it was there, of course. Their tacit understanding allowed it to remain in the house as long as it was kept out of sight and its contents did not disappear too rapidly. There were legitimate medicinal uses for it and, moreover, some occasions demanded celebration—Warren's graduation from medical school, his marriage, his move to Los Angeles to begin his residency. On the news of each of these occasions, Garnet grudgingly vouchsafed Tyson a glass at the dinner table. But there were other times, more solitary, where contemplation's melancholy demanded the bottle's assistance.

Tyson carried the bottle to the sink, leaving the basement door open. He took a glass from the dish rack and poured two fingers, twisted the cap on the bottle and started back towards the basement door. Halfway there, he hesitated, then continued—to close the door and return, still carrying the Seagram's.

He stalked into the living room, glanced evilly at the plastic-covered chairs and sofa before he sat in the chair, his chair, he had rescued. He took a sip of whiskey, grimacing a little as it went down, then settled back as the warm, fine glow spread from his stomach.

The trouble had come when he found himself loving Garnet enough to believe her without faults. By the time ignorance gave way to knowledge, it had become habit to defer to her. Now habit was all the years had left of love.

Even the game had been taken from him.

But with Jesse there was still hope. And in return for that hope, he would give the boy what he had promised—what he knew how to do as well as any man and had kept the knowledge of. He would have to remember to get out his glove and oil it. He would have to drive downtown for new baseballs.

Tyson kneaded his hand, imagining the feel of the leather and the sharp, woody smell of a new ball, imagining how he would work it in his hand, work the sweat and the dirt into it until he knew by the way it felt he could make it do anything. He stretched his right arm cautiously, listening for the soft click near his elbow, working it back and forth, spreading open his hand.

He was going to quit fooling around with Jesse in the boy's backyard, take him to the park. The boy already knew how to throw; it was time to teach him how to pitch. There was a difference—a pitcher was smart enough not to get himself in trouble. If he did, he could always get himself out.

Tyson cupped his hand, looking at his palm as if a ball were there. His first two fingers extended over the top of it, his thumb maintained steady pressure. He was no longer in the living room but back at the center of the diamond, the massed wave of voices swallowed in the still center of himself. His left shoulder pointed at the plate and he looked back from his stance, checking the position of the men in the outfield, then scanning the bleachers to see if Garnet had come.

He squinted, not seeing the television or the plastic-covered sofas and chairs, the pale pink artificial flowers in the vase beside Warren's graduation picture on the piano, but instead the plate and Spider Collins, whose glove had never let a pitch get away. And in front of Collins, the Babe, indolently knocking the bat against his spikes before he stepped back into the box.

Tyson nodded at Collins's signal and reared back, left leg kicking high in the air, bore down and released the ball, coming down into a crouch as he watched the ball bullet its way into Collins's glove.

He smiled to himself as he took another sip and the slow fire spread inside his belly. He still had it. Yes he did. And he could show the boy, show him the difference between a pitcher and a ballplayer who knew only how to throw.

9

the chimes sounded, breaking the soft surface of Garnet's slumber and she stirred, reluctant to leave sleep's dark embrace. The chimes came again, insisting their way into the dream that was already fading.

Garnet grumbled to herself, a mutter of vague dissent. With the heavy sense of duty that was her days' unwelcome companion, duty without name, duty endured, duty without end, she groped for the alarm clock. It was still dark in the bedroom, and the clock's dial glowed with a soft yellow light. The clock itself was silent. Eyes fully open now, Garnet looked around her, coming to terms with wakefulness. Tyson's side of the bed was empty. She called his name softly and heard his heavy footsteps downstairs.

The telephone, Garnet thought, and she sat up, the trickle of unease becoming a flood of fear. It was after midnight; a telephone call could only mean something had happened. Oh God, Garnet thought, because so much wrong roamed unchecked in the world—not the child. Not the child. Her thoughts raced, sudden and irrational, and Garnet prayed that it was not Warren, not the child. The prayer became an offer, a bargain. Immediately, Garnet was ashamed.

Still, something was wrong. She knew it. And out of her knowledge that life was nothing but unfair, Garnet steeled herself, praying now for the courage to accept what she could no longer prevent.

Leaning on one elbow, she strained to hear the deep murmur of Tyson's voice, waited in the darkened bedroom for him to come heavily up the stairs and pause just inside the doorway, hesitating before he came in and said, "Sugar?"

But his heavy tread did not come and now there was another voice, higher, thinner, and somehow familiar.

Garnet shook off the last remnants of sleep and sat up, one hand at her throat, eyes opening wide.

"Jesse?" she said hoarsely. "Jesse?"

"boy," tyson said. "What in the world you doing here? You know what time it is?"

Jesse pushed back his cap, grinning uncertainly under the porch light. He was dressed in a jacket, t-shirt, and blue jeans. He carried a small bag, his glove hooked over one of the handles. The ball was a bulge in his jacket pocket.

"You gonna let me in?" he asked.

Tyson nodded, stepping aside for the boy to enter. He closed the door and locked it, twisting the knob out of long habit to make sure.

"C'mon siddown," he said. "Then tell me what the hell's going on."

The boy followed him into the living room. He sat on the sofa, setting his bag on the floor. He reached down and unhooked the glove, then took out the ball. He pounded it once into the glove, looking around the living room, at the piano and the pictures on the mantel, before he turned to Tyson, grin more confident now.

Tyson settled into his chair, putting his feet up on the hassock. He reached down for the glass, hesitated, then took it from the floor.

"Awright," he said, "what's all this about?"

"I'm just doing what Garnet always said."

Tyson raised his eyebrows quizzically, and Jesse said, "She always said I could come stay with you if anything ever happened."

"She did?" Tyson chuckled. And then, as Jesse's grin faded, "C'mon, now son, things that bad at home?"

The boy said nothing. Tyson drank and belched softly.

"How you get here?" he asked. "It's a long ways to come by yourself."

"Took the bus. The driver told me where to transfer." Jesse looked at Tyson accusingly, as if he should have remembered, "I'll be twelve in September."

"Oh yeah. I almost forgot." He looked fondly at the boy, and Jesse sank back on the sofa, arms folded across his chest, the glove still on his hand.

"So tell me, how this all come up so sudden?"

"They said I couldn't see you again," Jesse said. "I told them where we went." He looked down at his scuffed sneakers, said, voice higher, words coming faster, "To get your money. It just slipped out. I tried to tell them nothing bad happened, but they wouldn't listen. They said I couldn't ever go out with you again. So I waited till they were sleeping, and then I crawled out the window."

Tyson knew it was wrong, that he should be stern, should tell the boy how it really was, but his face creased in a broad smile. The boy had a head on his shoulders. All the times he, Tyson, had brought him to the house, in his mother's station wagon or his own Chevrolet, calling off the names of the streets, pointing out the bus lines and the bus stops because a boy ought to know something more about the city where he lived than just his own neighborhood. The boy had a head on his shoulders—he had to give him that—and spunk besides. He was proud of him, but Tyson saw now what he was going to have to do. It was going to be hard.

"Jesse," he began, and then he heard Garnet's footsteps on the stairs.

"Tyson," she said, voice husky with sleep. "I must be dreaming, but I could have sworn I heard—" She stopped, eyes widening in fright and surprise as she saw the boy.

"Oh my Lord! It is you. Jesse, what in the world are you doing here?"

"You said I could come," Jesse said, unable to keep the plaintiveness out of his voice. He swung his legs, banging his heels against the sofa. "Remember? You said if things got too bad, I could always come and stay with you."

Garnet sighed and shook her head ruefully as she looked towards Tyson. Tyson grinned, enjoying her discomfort. She looked quickly away.

"Jesse," she began, "When I said that, I didn't mean..."

She stopped as the boy's shoulders slumped. And then he straightened, raising his head and looking at Garnet, eyes wet with betrayal. Still, he stuck out his lower lip, ready for the challenge. He kicked the sofa once.

"Well, it's too late now. I told them where we went, me and Tyson. They said I couldn't see him no more."

Tyson chuckled, cutting off Garnet's "Anymore—," and she whirled on him.

"What are you laughing at? It won't be you that has to pay for this. No sir. It's been sixteen years I worked for Mrs. Wilcox. Sixteen years—I remember the day this child was born. And now it's all gone. I just hope you're satisfied."

"Now, hol' on a minute," Tyson said. "I ain't the one told him..." Her face darkened with fury. "Sugar," he said. "Sugar..."

"Sugar? Hmmph! It's too late for that now."

"We don't have to tell them," Jesse said.

Garnet whirled on him, exasperation battling fondness on her face, before she sighed and made a little sound—tsst!—between her teeth.

"Jesse," she said, "you're as bad as he is. Now, what did I tell you about leaving your cap on when you come in the house? Take it off—it's just good manners. And if you don't stop knocking your heels against my good furniture..." Jesse tugged off the cap, pausing to scratch the top of his forehead before he set it on his knee. It was the way Tyson would have done it.

Garnet made the tsst! sound again, stifling a smile. She said, not looking at Tyson, "You know we need to call the police."

"*Po*-lice?" Tyson's voice cracked sharp with disbelief. "Woman, we don't need no *po*-lice messing 'round in this."

Jesse looked from face to face. Garnet stood in her dressing gown, hair in curlers, hands on her hips, glaring down at Tyson. Unable to meet her angry eyes, he slumped in his chair, looking down into his glass.

"None of this would ever have happened if you'd told him the truth," Garnet said, leveling a finger. "But no, you just had to go filling his little head with those damn lies about Babe Ruth. What happened wasn't good enough for you. You had to—"

Tyson nodded acquiescence, slumped on the edge of giving in as he had given in so many times before. He had been right; he saw that now. What he was going to have to do would be hard. He'd thought it was only telling the boy that, no matter what Garnet had said, he couldn't come to stay with them. But he'd seen what Garnet had—how the boy looked up to him, wearing his cap the way he wore his own, walking the way he walked. And so he was going to have tell Jesse the truth, the truth about what had happened with Babe Ruth.

"Woman," Tyson growled, "would you please be quiet. Please."

Garnet stopped in mid-sentence, mouth open, eyes wide with disbelief. Jesse looked away. Before Garnet could gather herself for another assault, he said, "Go call his momma."

"Tyson," Jesse pleaded. "Tyson..."

"Go call his momma," Tyson said.

Garnet glared at him a long moment, as if calculating what she would do once the boy was gone and it was just the two of them. Finally, she went out into the hall.

"Tyson," Jesse said. "What'd she mean? She's just mad, isn't she?"

Tyson shushed him. Garnet was dialing. After a moment, she said, too brightly, "Mrs. Wilcox? Garnet Odom. Sorry to trouble you so late— Yes, ma'am, I know what time it is, but I knew you'd want me to call. It's about Jesse… He's here. Just a few minutes ago. Excuse me? No, I don't know how. No, no, he's fine."

When she came back, she said, "They'll be right over."

"Good." Tyson leaned over for the bottle. Garnet frowned disapprovingly. He poured two fingers, and then a third, capped the bottle and set it down again.

"Garnet," he said, "go upstairs and bring me my scrapbook."

She looked at him, head cocked, the look that said enough was enough—he should know better than to continue with this foolishness.

"Ain't got time to argue with you," Tyson said. "Boy's parents be here soon. And I know you know where it is."

Garnet pinned him with eyes of fire, and then she stalked out of the living room. Tyson heard her footsteps mounting the stairs, heard her walking back towards what had once been Warren's room at the back of the house. He took a long swallow of his drink, then set down his glass, looking at the boy.

"Jesse," he said gently, "son. All those times I told you 'bout me and Babe Ruth… She's right—I got to tell you what really happened."

Jesse stared. And then he shook his head, lips trembling, eyes wet, face wide with confusion. He looked like something bad had happened and it might be his fault, but he wasn't sure yet. Like he'd come up the stairs on his way to a part of the house he wasn't supposed to go to and put out his foot expecting to find a step except there wasn't one, and so he'd fallen and hurt himself, but he wasn't going to cry.

"You told me," Jesse said, voice high and thin. "You struck him out. Three times. You told me."

Tyson nodded. "Jesse," he said, but it was as if he had not spoken.

"You told me! So many times, I can see it—you out there on the mound, taking your cap off and wiping your forehead with the back of your hand. You used to do that sometimes, when you got tired, sneak a little sweat on the ball to make it do tricks."

Tyson chuckled.

"Yes sir, I would. But just every once in a while. Spitter's an old man's pitch, and I wasn't never that old a ballplayer."

On the edge of the sofa, Jesse looked at Tyson, searching his face. Tyson said, "Shhh. Hush now. I promised I'd tell you." He chuckled, holding up the glass to the light, inspecting the rich whiskey amber. "Some things take time, like this liquor. Imagine before he finally got it right, man made a whole lot wasn't hardly fit to drink."

So they waited, the man and the boy, listening to the clock on the mantelpiece ticking away the seconds and the sound of Garnet's footsteps upstairs. When she came down again she had changed out of her dressing gown and combed out her hair. She was carrying the scrapbook.

"Give it here," Tyson said.

It was thick and heavy, smelled of dry, dusty, crumbling paper. And yet the leather was supple and smooth, as if someone had been caring for it all the long years. Tyson looked at Garnet, but she was bent over Jesse, hand on his shoulder.

"Hungry?" Garnet said. "You want something to eat?"

The boy shook his head. His eyes had not left Tyson. Tyson said, almost to himself, "Been a long time since I seen this. C'mere, Jesse. Take a look."

The boy rose from the sofa and came reluctantly, still holding onto his glove. He stood beside Tyson, looking over his shoulder.

"That's the time I had me a no-hitter going into the ninth in Nashville." Tyson pointed, and Jesse nodded. "Dixie Dukes at the Elite Giants. Then Oscar Charleston got a single. Stole second, too, before I put out the side."

Across the room, Garnet sat on the sofa, hands clenched in her lap.

"Huh," she said softly to herself. "Huh!"

Jesse glanced at her before he looked back at the scrapbook. Tyson turned the page and the paper crumbled, a brittle brown flake falling onto the knee of his pajamas.

"And this was Atlanta. Lemme see...nineteen and twenty-nine. Or was it thirty? Garnet, you remember?"

"I don't know anything about you and Atlanta," she said tightly. "Papa had relatives there, but I haven't seen them in years." She sniffed. "But I do know about you and Babe Ruth."

"Thirty-one," Tyson said decisively. "Nineteen and thirty-one, because it was the same year we played at the old stadium they fixin' to tear down now. Same year I pitched to the Babe."

Garnet said, "Huh!" and Jesse said, "Wow! You went all over. Look, Garnet—Mobile, Alabama; Tupelo, Mississippi; Kansas City; Chicago. Here's one from New York."

The plastic-covered sofa squeaked under Garnet's weight, but she said nothing.

"Philadelphia," Tyson said. "New Jersey. All the way up to Canada. Coulda gone to Mexico, maybe even Cuba, hadn't messed up my arm."

"Wow," Jesse said again, and Tyson looked up from the book to Jesse's face, seeing himself through the boy's wondering eyes and remembering what it was like. He was not quite thirty, young enough, strong enough, so that the long rides on the bus that was always breaking down were nothing. But that last long, hot summer, the summer the league went under and the Dukes had had to barnstorm or go home and go hungry, had been the worst. He couldn't remember ever feeling cool, not even way up North at night with the bus windows rolled down. Down South, in between the small towns, they prayed the restaurant on their side of town that they remembered from last season was still there. If it wasn't, they swallowed their pride and went where they could, caps in hand to the window in the back where colored were served.

The ball parks were warped clapboard with roach-infested changing rooms when there was someplace to change. Most times, they dressed on the bus before trotting out onto the diamond. The white folks sat in the stands while the colored claimed the sun-drenched bleachers. A few minutes tossing the ball around the infield before the umpire yelled, "Play ball!" and then everything they'd endured to get to that moment fell away and time began again, nine new innings to get it right.

"It wasn't all good, Jesse," Tyson said slowly.

Garnet said, "Amen!" and got up to stand in the window, turning her back on them. She held the curtain so she could see outside.

"So why'd you keep doing it?"

Tyson shrugged and took a sip of whiskey, washing it around his mouth before he swallowed.

"Was hard times for a man like me, Negro man didn't have no schooling. Wasn't nothing else I could do. 'Cept work my daddy's land or make some other strainy kind of living." He dipped his head and smiled almost shyly. "'Sides, wasn't a thing I loved better than playing ball."

That was it, what he'd always known, but never said, not in all these years. Men like Spider Collins and Preacher Bates already knew, and so there was no need to speak of it. Even Lamarr Jenkins, watching the world go by from behind his barber chair, understood. Which was why the barber had said nothing, even though he'd looked at him with a hint of pity, the way he might have looked at a man who'd taken to wearing his hair as if he were twenty years younger. He, Tyson, had loved the game. Why else would he have put up with all that came along with it, knowing the whole time there wasn't a chance in hell he could make the majors where the real money was? He'd loved it, was sorry now the long, cramped, sweaty bus rides were over and done with, sorry he'd never slump sleepless in the hard seat again, listening to Frog Richmond and Willie Brown chivvying Mule in the back, while Cortez Pettigrew hummed a blues, and Spider Collins and Preacher Bates argued about who was the best hitter the Negro Leagues had ever seen. And Willis Mitchell's sad whiskey voice coming from up front, remembering the curve he had once had or the way the ball had soared across the sky when he'd hit his grand slam, his only home run in some twenty years in the league.

"I loved it," Tyson said. "God's truth, Jesse—I loved it."

"Better than you did any woman," Garnet said bitterly, still peering through the curtains. "No woman could have come close."

Tyson looked over at her shamefaced because he could not deny the truth she'd spoken. But she had understood, once, long ago before it had gone wrong between them. She had; he knew it.

Outside, a car went by, slowing as it passed the house.

"Switch on the porch light, sugar," Tyson said, before he turned the page. "Now, this here's the one you saw this afternoon in the barbershop, Jesse. Me and the Babe shaking hands."

He looked the boy in the eye, readying himself.

"But I got something to tell you, Jesse. Man to man. Square bidness." Tyson paused, longing for the whiskey that would make it easier. "It didn't happened the way I told you. I never struck out Babe Ruth."

The boy held his eye for a moment. And then he backed away from Tyson, face stricken.

"You lied," he said. "Just like Garnet said. You lied."

"Naw, son, I didn't lie. I just—"

"I knew something was wrong, the way Mr. Lamarr looked at you in the barbershop. You probably never even pitched to Babe Ruth."

"No," Garnet said. "That's not true, Jesse. He did."

Tyson's face creased in surprise, but the car was in front of the house now. He heard the engine shut down and the doors open before they slammed shut. He did not have much time.

"Jesse," he said, "son, I might have said some things wasn't exactly so, but I didn't lie. Least not a lie meant to hurt nobody or claim something wasn't mine." He stopped, looking at the boy before he took his feet down from the hassock. "Lemme tell you how it really happened and you can make up your own mind. Siddown. Gon' take a little while."

The boy looked at him, lower lip poked out, eyes wet with tears. "Jesse," Tyson said softly, almost pleading. After a long moment, Jesse came to the hassock. He sat unwillingly, holding himself away from Tyson. Ignoring Garnet's scowl, Tyson reached down and refilled his glass.

"'Twas an exhibition game," Tyson began, taking his time with the familiar opening. "Just like I always told you. See, in them days, white and colored didn't play in the same leagues. Shoot, some places down South it was against the law even for us to be on the same field at the same time. But they knew we was as good as they was, and sometimes after the season was over, the white owners'd put together a team to go all over the country. Played the colored clubs, places it wasn't against the law.

"That's how it come to happen. Babe Ruth's Major League All Stars 'gainst the Dixie Dukes of Washington, D.C. Now you know who I had behind me."

Jesse held himself stiffly, not moving at all.

"Mule Hastings was in center," Tyson began. "Anderson Turner was in right field. His twin brother Wilkins played shortstop. Now, let's see..."

Tyson waited, long enough to understand Jesse would not complete the lineup.

"Tony Spinks third," he said, "Preacher Bates at second, Cortez Pettigrew left field. And Frog Richmond was playing first."

The doorbell rang and Garnet rose quickly from the sofa.

"Lookahere," Tyson said. "Don't he look just like a frog? And this here's Mule. Called him that 'cause he was as ugly as one. But they shoulda called him Thoroughbred, 'cause that's what he was—boy saved us more than once that day with them long legs." Tyson sighed and shook his head. "Shame what happened to him. Just a shame."

"Jesse," the boy's father said. He was all forehead and glasses, a wisp of blond hair pasted down across his naked skull. "You all right, son?"

His wife knelt to put her arms around Jesse.

"Thank God you're all right," she said, but Jesse was already twisting away.

Mr. Wilcox bared his teeth, an offering to keep the world from getting too close instead of a smile. His wife looked up at Tyson through his pajama-clad knees. "Ma'am," he said pleasantly. She colored and rose quickly to her feet. Garnet stood beside the boy's father, wringing her hands.

"You shouldn't have left like that, son," Mr. Wilcox said. "Your mother was worried. That wasn't too considerate, was it, Jesse?"

Tyson cleared his throat.

"Whyn't y'all have a seat?" he offered. "Me and the boy's talking, but it won't take but a little while." He turned back to Jesse. "Like I was sayin', shame about what happened to Mule. He sure could cover some ground on them long legs, but at the end when he got that cancer, wasn't nothin' could help him atall."

Irritation wrinkled Mr. Wilcox's face before he drove it away with a smile.

"Jesse needs to go home now," he said. "But thank you—"

"That's right," Mrs. Wilcox said, a brittleness in her voice that said she was used to getting what she wanted. "But thank you so much for making sure he was all right."

"Now hol' on," Tyson said. "Where I come from, folks usually accepts an invitation to sit down. Man welcomes you in his house, you don't just rush off. 'Less you truly don't care for his company."

"Now wait just a minute—" Mr. Wilcox said, his voice hardening. Tyson cut him off, raising one big brown hand.

"Boy come all this way by himself to talk to me, I reckon he old enough to hear what I got to say. You folks sit down. Want, you can go in the kitchen. Garnet, maybe they want some coffee or something."

"Tyson," Mr. Wilcox said. "Mr. Odom—"

Garnet laid her hand on his arm.

"I'm sorry," she said. "But when he gets this way, I can't do a thing with him."

"Sinclair," Mrs. Wilcox said, "are you going to let him—" but Tyson was looking at Jesse as if the two of them were alone and they had not been interrupted.

"Night before, Doc Blanton asked me did I feel I could pitch," he said.

Jesse's parents exchanged glances, his mother's eyes cold and furious above a smile of bemused tolerance. After a moment, they followed Garnet to the sofa. Mrs. Wilcox glanced around the living room, eyes widening at the baby grand piano and the open sheet music—Mozart—before she sat down.

"Told Doc no, didn't believe I could," Tyson said. "Done pitched twice in four days, and the only rest I had was on the bus, coming east through Virginia. My arm was hurtin', and I'm thinking I got to take care of myself—wasn't nobody else gon' look out for me. I could live with not going to Mexico, but I sure 'nough wanted to play colored league ball in the spring."

Outside, there was a noise like faint applause or the dying rush of the crowd's cheer. Tyson paused, straining to hear—it was only a bus on the dark city streets.

"Well," he said, "Doc knew we didn't have more than a fifty-fifty chance with anybody else. Ol' Willie Brown didn't have nothing but a spitball, and Norvell Akins—shoot, Norvell didn't hardly have no control at all. But Doc, he understood and I got to give the man credit—he backed me when he knew Mr. Bloodsworth just might fire him if we lost.

"And we did all right with Willie Brown. That old man had a spitter couldn't be hit. We was up two to nothing after one, then had us two more runs in the third to make it four. Fourth inning's when it begin to fall apart. Willie got caught using the spitter, and Norvell had to come in. And he hadn't had no more control that last half the season than a fat lady walkin' past a candy store."

Tyson paused, rolling his glass in his cradled hands.

"I ain't gon' stretch it out, Jesse; I'm just gon' tell you what happened. Looked like Norvell wasn't gon' do too bad at first. Mule hit his second home run of the day in the fifth, though it cost him ten dollars, 'cause Doc Blanton given him strict instructions to bunt. But Norvell give up three runs in the fifth and sixth, and we was looking at a five to three ballgame.

"Well, sir, Norvell loaded the bases in the seventh, and Babe Ruth was due up. That's when I told Doc put me in. Doc asked me was I sure. Said hell yeah—'scuse me, Miz Wilcox. That was the first time I pitched to Babe Ruth. Got him out too."

A slow grin spread across Jesse's face despite his attempt to check it.

"Didn't say I struck him out, son. No sir. Ruth hit a grounder straight at me, and I threw him out. But you ain't got to throw three strikes to get a man out—way I threw that ball, wasn't nothing he could do 'cept put it on the ground." Tyson tapped his temple with one finger. "That's pitching, son, that's pitching."

He looked at the boy to make sure he understood, and then he sipped from his glass.

"Anyway, I got us out of the seventh and in the eighth I set them boys down in order—one, two, three. Awright, now it's our half of the ninth, and remember, we still up by two. If we coulda just got us a couple—Lord!—things mighta been different. But we didn't and it turned out the way it did, no matter how much I wish it hadn't been so. We went down, one, two, three—Tony Spinks, Frog, and Turner. Anderson, not Wilkins. Hit him a long drive, but he got nailed at second."

"So now it was up to you," Jesse said. "And you faced six men in the ninth. Giacometti, Stones, Doerr, Tolliver, Wakowski. And Ruth."

"You got a head for names," Tyson said. "Got every one right. Giacometti, Stones, Doerr, Tolliver, Wakowski, and Ruth." He ticked them off on his fingers. "Six men. Me and Collins was working together good. Real good. Had Giacometti ready to go down on strikes, and then he just dribbled one into the infield and was safe at first. Stones bunted and I threw him out, but I knew that was it, I had to bear down now because I was looking at the top of the order.

"First man's Richie Doerr. Loaded the count on him, then he hit it to Spinks. Tony had a little trouble—Doerr hit that ball hard, but might could it bounced off a stone. Anyway, that's two men on, and one man out, and I'm mad. My arm was hurting, but I give Tolliver three fastballs. Three fastballs, and everyone of them was a strike."

Tyson grinned, shaking his head to himself.

"Two more," Jesse said softly. "Wakowski. Then Ruth."

"That's right. Had been any other day, any other time, maybe I woulda gotten Wakowski and not had to face Ruth. But my arm was all used up—I figured I had me ten, maybe twelve, pitches left, and wasn't none of them that good. So I walked Wakowski. Wasn't on purpose—I just didn't have no stuff."

Tyson tipped the glass to his mouth and swallowed the last of his whiskey. He set the glass down carefully on the floor beside his chair.

"Awright. Bases loaded and here come the Babe, a great big old fat man, look like a barrel with legs. Soon as he hoisted that bat on his shoulders, the crowd started yelling so loud I couldn't hardly hear myself think. 'Easy, Tyson,' I told myself. 'He ain't nothing but a man.' Ol' Spider called for the curve twice, and I dipped my head to say awright. Wasn't no use tryna burn it by the Babe.

"Well, I threw it down there, and each time that ball broke like a curve of mine never broke before. Now I'm behind, two-and-oh. Got the ball back, I looked at it—there's a little cut near the seams. Spider'd do that sometimes I was having trouble—cut the ball with a bottle cap he hid in his glove. Didn't want none of that this time. Wanted to face the Babe man to man."

Jesse nodded his approval.

"Man to man," he said. "Just you and him, Tyson."

"Well, I tol' the umpire gimme a new ball. Threw it down again, fastball this time. Blew it down past the Babe so he couldn't hardly get a look at it. Strike one."

Garnet sat primly, hands on her knees, looking away towards the window behind Tyson's chair. She nodded, but he did not see her.

"Awright. Two and one, and the Babe ain't even got a piece of the ball yet. Spider called for the curve. Now, Jesse, God's truth—that's the only call I question. That curve so sweet, I knew I couldn't never throw another like it, not if I lived to be a hundred years." Tyson shook his head, laughter easy and indolent. "Only God ever made a sweeter curve, and that was on a woman's body."

Mrs. Wilcox sniffed disapprovingly, but a smile flickered over Garnet's face before her lips tightened back into the straight line.

"Umpire called ball three. So I give him the fastball again. And the Babe jumped on it, swung that bat and found himself teetering and tottering, arms wrapped 'round like he was giving himself a hug."

Jesse laughed, and Garnet said, "Strike two."

Tyson turned his head slowly in surprise.

"Nobody made a sound," Garnet said. "It was so quiet in that stadium, Cook said you could hear a mouse walking on cotton."

"Full count, now," Tyson said, still looking at Garnet. "Bases loaded. Spider called for the curve three times, and each time the Babe just nicked it foul. Next time Spider called for the curve, I said no, I was gon' give him the fastball. Burn him, see, show him a good ol' North Carolina country fastball. Maybe I didn't have but one more pitch left, but I was sure 'nuff gon' use it to strike out Babe Ruth.

"Now Spider, he don't want the fastball. Had to shake off the sign twice before he shrug and say awright. Ballpark still quiet, and I'm out there all alone taking my time, getting my strength back for that last pitch."

"You got him," Jesse said. "I knew it. You got him, didn't you?"

Tyson smiled ruefully. "Now whose story is this? Whose story is it?"

"Yours, Tyson. It's your story."

"Awright, then. So lemme finish it my own way. 'Cause it ain't important whether I got him or not. That ain't what I want you to take with you when you go home. What I'm trying to tell you, son, is life can be hard. And sometimes a man don't get what he wants, the things he works for. So he tries to hol' on, tries so hard he forgets why it was so doggone important he was ready to give up everything he had in the first place. If he's lucky, he figures out what he done wrong. Then, if it ain't too late, he might get the chance to go back and find the truth and tell it. You understand what I'm tryna say, Jesse?"

The boy shook his head, and Tyson forced a weary smile.

"Never mind," he said sadly. "You will. You will. Anyway, I'm gon' put all I got left on this fastball, burn it past the Babe if I can't sneak it by him. I waited a long time, waited till the umpire was 'bout ready to tell me to pitch or vacate the mound. And when I was ready, I kicked back—I swear, never kicked so high in my life—and when I let go, that ball left my hand like a bullet."

It was Jesse's father who broke the silence that followed.

"Did you get him?" he asked. "Did you get him?"

"Felt a pain shoot up my arm," Tyson said, as if he had not heard, as if it were no longer important. "Like somebody stuck a hot knife in my elbow. And I heard it pop. Just like that—pop!"

He looked sorrowfully at Jesse. The boy looked back at him, face grave and serious.

"When I heard that bat hit the ball, I knew that ball was gone. Mule took off on them long legs, but everybody knew it wasn't no use. All anybody could do was watch it go, clear out the stadium."

No one said anything. Tyson closed the scrapbook and laid it carefully on the floor.

"That ball was gone," he said. "That ball was gone."

Unnoticed, the ball fell from Jesse's glove and rolled towards the sofa. His father bent to pick it up. The boy sat studying Tyson for a long time, brow wrinkled, before he spoke.

"Why'd you do it?" he asked, voice as forlorn as if he'd been there, had sat stunned as Ruth rounded the bases and came trotting into the knot of waiting All Stars while the Dukes shambled off the field. "You never pitched again. Why'd you do it?"

Tyson shrugged.

"I had to, son. I had to."

"No you didn't. You coulda just said no and sat on the bench."

"Coulda," Tyson admitted. "Doc wouldn'ta said nothin', nobody else neither. Maybe I just wasn't thinking straight."

But that wasn't it. He'd known what he was doing when he'd gone to Doc. And he'd wanted to jam the ball past Ruth, had wanted to show every white man in the park—no, every man—that the Dukes were as good as any team in the majors. Because there was the All Star—Doerr? Giacometti? He'd forgotten which one—who'd come up to the Dukes' bat boy and said, "Lemme rub this little nigger's head for luck."

But that wasn't it either.

The truth was, he had done it for love. For Mule and for Frog, for Spider and Anderson and Wilkins Turner, for Preacher Bates and all the rest whose names and faces had faded in his memory. For Garnet, in case her parents had relented and she'd come and was watching. The truth was, he had done it for love.

"I told you," Tyson said. "We couldn't get to play on their teams. But I didn't do it to show 'em. I did it—" He stopped, embarrassed at what he might reveal that a man kept hidden because to name it was to risk losing it. "I did it because they needed me. Dixie Dukes was my team. They needed me."

The boy and the man looked into each other's eyes a long time, as some secret knowledge passed wordlessly between them, and then Jesse nodded, his face clearing.

"You got the call," Jesse said. "And you went out there and did your best. Just like you always tell me—do your best."

"That's right," Tyson said. "That's right."

Jesse stood then and came to him, putting his arms around Tyson, the glove behind Tyson's neck, as the boy embraced the man. Tyson's arms rose to encircle him.

"But you can still teach me?" Jesse said urgently. "We don't have to go hard. We can take it easy, Tyson."

"He can," Mr. Wilcox said. "If you really want him to."

Jesse pulled away to look at his father. His father stood to hand him the ball.

"I mean it," he said.

"Sinclair," Mrs. Wilcox said, smiling her brittle smile.

"Your mother's right," he said. "You should ask Mr. Odom if he'd like to."

"Tyson," Jesse said. "Tyson. You hear that? You gonna teach me, Tyson?"

"All he remembers," Garnet said. "But it's way after midnight, child. Go on home now. Need to get your rest if you're going to be a ballplayer."

"That's right," Tyson said, shaking himself as if rousing from sleep. He reached out to tousle the boy's hair. "We'll take it real slow. Got to build up your arm before you can start throwing bullets."

"Promise?" Jesse said. He tugged on his cap, setting it just right, the way Tyson would set it, but he was looking at his father.

His father said, "That's a promise, son. C'mon, now—let's go home."

Garnet saw them to the door. Tyson remained slumped in his chair. They were talking, but he was no longer curious about what she might be telling them. It was done with. He felt old and tired. It was done with.

"i told them I wouldn't be in on Monday," Garnet said as she came into the living room. She went to the fireplace, stood before it, arms wrapped around her body, as if she was cold and the artificial logs were giving off heat. "She can mail me the money for the last two weeks, now that she knows where I live."

"It's honest work," Tyson said emptily. "I'd worry 'bout you at home by yourself. Neighborhood gone down so far, it ain't funny."

"Hmmmph!" Garnet sniffed. And then, "We'll see how long she can get along by herself."

Tyson smiled for the first time since he had finished the story.

"Yeah."

Rubbing her shoulder as if it ached, Garnet sighed and went to the piano. She sat, as if about to open it and play. And for a moment, seated on the bench, back straight, arms extended, face set in concentration as she readied herself, she was that girl again, and it was like the time Tyson had heard her that Sunday evening at Providence, the time she had shown him there was things she, too, had that called to her, called to her the way the game called to him. And when she had come to him in his room at the Whitelaw Hotel after that game, she'd given him those things and he had taken them as if they were his due, taken them past the possibility of her ever having them be hers again.

Garnet sat as if she were going to play, but she only reached out and drew her finger across the top of the piano, as if checking for dust. Tyson said, "I'm sorry."

She looked at him, surprised.

"What for?"

He shrugged, lost for words to say it.

"I did what I could, what a man's supposed to," Tyson said haltingly. "But I couldn't give you what you really wanted. What you was supposed to have. If I hadn't wanted you so bad, if you hadn't come to me that night at the Whitelaw..." He shrugged. "You might coulda done all them things you was called to do."

9

garnet sat motionless, head turned to hide her face, so still so long, it was as if she had not heard. When she raised her head to look at him, her face was shiny with tears.

"All these years," she said. "I just wanted to hear you say it."

"I know," he said, and she said, "Oh, Tyson, Tyson, Tyson," thinking, not of him, but of how it had been after her father had died and she had finally been allowed back to the house in LeDroit Park. She'd gone to sit in the parlor with her mother, who seemed frail and diminished, disoriented at finding herself alone.

"Things haven't been easy for you," her mother had said, and she'd nodded, torn between the need to admit Tyson's shortcomings and the need to preserve what was left of her pride.

"Why didn't you come to us?" her mother said, and she'd seen in her mother's face a quality of knowing that could be learned only from living.

"But Mother," she'd said, "what could you have done?" and in her mother's answering sad smile knew that same knowledge was plain on her own face, that she had crossed over some line of demarcation and was no longer child or truly even daughter.

"Oh, Tyson," she said now. "It wasn't all yours to bear, no matter how much I might have acted like it." Garnet laughed flatly. "Maybe I just used you as an excuse. Maybe I was scared I wasn't going to be good enough, and I'd wind up teaching school or playing behind a church choir the rest of my life."

She laughed again, unable to keep a touch of bitterness out of her laugh, before she took a handkerchief from the sleeve of her dress and blew her nose.

Tyson said nothing, only looked at her, brows knitted. It hurt to look at her, and yet he could not look aside. Garnet crumpled the handkerchief and tucked it away. Her face was still sad, but her clear eyes met his gaze.

She came to him then, came to sit on the arm of his chair, taking his hand with a little smile on her face. After a moment, she moved to sit on his lap.

"It's late, old lady," Tyson said, and she tossed her head, as if to say, So what if it is?, a sweet motion that conjured up her head tossed back in easy laughter that same way a long time before, a glimpse of the lithe brown girl hiding inside her heaviness. And all the other seasons of skin and body—the slow swelling and her fecund ungainly grace when she bore Warren, her skin pale yellow in spring, browning in summer, the rich undertones of red in fall, paling again in winter.

Tyson reached up to touch her cheek, brushing away a gray curl.

Garnet smiled, the old teasing smile that one minute offered lips for kissing—lips just as quickly drawn away—the old teasing smile that said he might have gotten her to go walking with him, but she was different, and was he man enough to find out how much?

Now Garnet pressed herself to him, her face against his neck.

"I've got something to tell you," she said, and in her voice there was longing and hopelessness and defiance born of that hopelessness, and something else unnameable that had always left him confused and guilty, on the verge of stuttering, "What did I do?"

Garnet said, "I heard your arm."

It took him a moment to understand.

"You was there? You never told me."

She nodded against his neck.

"The tickets you left? Papa gave them to Cook. I made her give me one. We all went—Cook, her husband, their boys. They were good seats. Any closer, and we would have been right on the field. And I heard your arm, right when you threw that last time."

"Shush," Tyson said. "It's over and done with, sugar. It don't matter now. C'mon—it's late. Let's go on up to bed."

She moved, as if about to rise, but only to pull away, to look at him, sadness and pity mixed in her face. "All right," she said. "All right."

Garnet walked beside him as they went up, holding his hand as if he were an old man who needed help on the stairs. She waited in the doorway while he turned off the hall light. Together, they went in, and he sat heavily on the side of the bed. Garnet undressed, hung her frock neatly on a hanger and put it away in the closet. Clad in nightgown, she went to stand in front of the mirror, took up a curler, then put it down.

"It sounded just like somebody breaking a stick," Garnet said, looking at her own reflection in the mirror. "I bit my lip so hard the blood ran.

"Nobody else seemed to notice. And it was so loud with all those people cheering, it was like I was all by myself. You know how you think things when you're all alone? Tyson, I knew it was wicked, but I let myself think what I'd wanted the whole time.

"I was glad it happened," she said. "You wouldn't ever be able to pitch again, and you'd have to leave the road and settle down. You weren't going to Mexico. But it wasn't meanness, Tyson; selfishness, maybe, but it wasn't meanness."

She came to him, then, kneeling by the side of the bed and taking his hand, looking up at him with pleading eyes.

"I wanted you, Tyson. I wanted you. And to keep everything else I already had because I wouldn't have to give it up to have you. I was ready to, but when you hurt your arm it meant I could have you, and not just letters and a phone call before you had to run to get a sandwich because they were almost done filling the bus with gas. I wanted you."

Tyson reached to pull her up, to draw her to him, to hold her. "I know," he said. "I know."

but of course he had not, had not been certain at all. And for a moment, lost in misery as crippling as the pain that had ruined his good throwing arm, Tyson almost believed she had planned it, caused it out of the fierceness of her desire. If only, if only… But all the wishing and hoping, all the world's crying and cursing could not change what had happened in an instant, leaving him no possibility of ever going back.

Would it have been better to have had it happen over time? The way it had happened to Frog Richmond—a slow wearing down, so that it seemed just yesterday Frog had been able to cover the ground, judging the flight of the ball as he ran, arriving not even breathing hard to meet it with his glove. And then one day the mind willed, but the body stumbled, and Frog, a step late and a jump short, woke each morning knowing a little more of what he had taken for granted was gone forever.

"I had to tell you," Garnet said. "Because you were always there. Things were hard before I went to work, but you always found a way. What we needed, we had; what we couldn't get, we did without. But all I ever had to do was ask. You provided."

"'Course I did," Tyson said, voice thick and heavy. "You was my only jewel." He did not know what else to say. If that last pitch had been different, he might never have known how much she wanted him for himself.

"You've been good to me," she said. "All these years, and you never complained. Well, not much, anyway."

"You're a good woman."

"Well..."

and so garnet stands and crosses to her side of the bed. In a little while, by mutual, unspoken consent, they move towards one another. The curves of their bodies fit, hip to thigh, chest to breast. The house is still. Outside, for a moment, the restless city sleeps. They have come this far together; it is not for them to say how much farther there is to go. But in that time, they have weathered and worn against each other, reaching an accommodation, as a tree establishes its roots around a stone, or water wears away rock. They have each other, for better, for worse, and each of them knows it.

Perhaps they will make love, as they have not for some time, skin against skin, flesh against flesh, finding salvation in surrender. Things will change, a little perhaps. Only the morning will tell. But that does not matter. For they hold each other. And right now, neither is alone.

CAROLINA IS DANCING

Carolina is dancing, soft and slow, stick legs in mesh stockings, buckles on tap shoes winking in the spotlight. She shim-sham-shimmies across the floor with detached enthusiasm, breaks into a split, and grins. She turns her back and wiggles her bottom, ancient buttocks heaving in tight white shorts.

Behind her, Ray, presiding at the bass, nods, yes sir, to himself. The white pick-up drummer smiles foolishly, not knowing what to make of it. And the piano player, whose name really is Chopin, has his head down as he monotonizes the blues.

Carolina is dancing, and the people seated in the redwood-and-Day-Glo restaurant ask themselves why. They came to hear Ray and Chopin, perhaps even Lola, if they were lucky. But there she is, Carolina, stamping out time to the white boy's uneven drumbeat, skin the same color of the black wig askew under her white top hat; pointed tips of rhinestone glasses give her demon eyes. She grins, shows missing teeth, nose and chin almost meeting in sunken face. Crazy nigger hoodoo woman. They came for Lola, Lola with her voice as strong and as rich as the young Ella's. "Satin Doll" is her signature song and, if she has not yet quite made it her own, there is always in her voice the promise she will one day. There she is now at a table up front, cool powdered light brown face over a lace blouse, cross-legged in knee-high boots. She laughs when one of the men at the table whispers in her ear.

Carolina, almost done with her tired tent-show hoochie-koo, extends one leg, rippling mundane thigh muscles. Someone whistles and her grin comes of its own accord. Lola laughs again and holds out another cigarette. The same man lights it immediately.

The drummer scatters one last careless roll and sounds the cymbal, Chopin's chords are empty echoes. Carolina hangs her head and genial Ray grabs the microphone: "Carolina, la-dies and gentlemen. The inimitable Miss Carolina."

There is tepid applause, like the shank of night and a cigarette at the bottom of a cup of abandoned coffee. Carolina bows, straightens, taking off the white top hat. She sets it on Lola's table.

"One more," she says. "One more song. And don't none of y'all be shy about comin' up to put sumpin' in this."

The band begins without her, and she turns, stamping her foot until they fall in, letting them go on until she is sure they have gotten it. She holds the microphone close to weathered lips, rubbing the words against her raspy voice. She sings:

Give you anything you want babe,
Just so long you comin' back to me.

She sings the lines again, and then:

Take all the money out my pocket,
'N' give you all the clothes off my back.

"Not much texture," Lola says, and the man beside her nods.

If Carolina hears, she goes on despite the words. They are not important, and who give a damn about texture anyway? Once, she sings, in the back room of a blind pig in Galveston, I made a big buck from Shrevesport lay down his straight razor. There was an American flag embedded in its mother-of-pearl handle, and he began to cry for his momma. I made the thunder roll and the lightning flash. I stole the gold teeth from the open mouth of a sleeping high-yellow undertaker because he would not leave his wife. My heart was young and foolish but, for a little while, I rode the wind.

The man beside her leans closer, but Lola pulls away. Chopin takes a solo, eyes closed now, face shiny with sweat agony. The chords are whorehouse laughter, as ornate as the pattern on a gambler's vest. Someone gets up to put a dollar in Carolina's hat. Others follow. Ray plays what he has always known. Carolina sings:

Men, you better love your woman,
'Cause you hate to see her go.
Men, you better love your woman,
'Cause you hate to see her go.
And when you do mistreat her,
You know it's bound to show.

"Yes, yes, yes," Ray says, shaking his head, and even the drummer seems to have it now. The band finishes and Carolina takes one last bow, leaves taking the hat full of bills. And before she goes, in acknowledgment or propitiation, Lola too takes a bill from the table and puts it in the hat.

A FEW GOOD MEN

The way the men in the shop start talking about women that Saturday night is this: The telephone rings once more for Speed, and Lamarr Jenkins, whose shop it is, heaves a heavy sigh of exasperation. Even if Speed were not the newest barber, it would still make sense for his chair to be near the pay telephone and the back room. Since Speed came to work at the shop three weeks before, the telephone has rung for him with the regularity of a factory whistle or the landlord's knock. Always, it is some young girl, a different sweet, young voice each time, asking tentatively for Speed. Always, Speed talks to her, his back to his customer, his own voice pitched low and soothing. This time, when Speed finally returns to the head he has been cutting, Jenkins scans the line of men waiting in the chairs underneath the mirrors against the wall. And then, without looking at Speed, Jenkins asks if Speed thinks about cutting hair when he is getting some. Speed says no—a man ought to keep his mind on the task at hand. Jenkins says fine—from now on, stop thinking about getting pussy when you in here supposed to be cutting hair.

After the laughter dies down, old Mr. Perkins, over whose half-bald head Jenkins has been aimlessly wielding his clippers, rouses himself long enough to say, "Boy must be working two or three jobs. Got to be, all them women he got."

Speed grins. A razor-thin man, he has a wicked Ike Turner goatee and a sleek otter's head of slicked-back hair.

"Who you think I am?" Speed asks. "Hubble?"

Hubble, the second barber, ignores it and continues placidly grooming his customer. Hubble is a big man. Though he does not drink, there is a whiskey sadness about him, an amiable alcoholic diffidence. Speed snorts and shakes his head.

"I got one rule," he says, "and one rule only. I live by it. If they don't pay, I don't play."

"Shee-it," says A.B. Prudhomme, a Louisianan known for obvious reasons as Seventh Street Red. "You pay. We all do. One way or another, you pay. Don't nobody give up nothing for nothing. Especially these black gals out here."

"Thass right," Mr. Perkins says over the chorus of assents from the men waiting. Speed says, "You right. Somea these young girls they got out here, you got to be careful. They'll try to game you in a minute."

Doc, an English teacher at the high school, looks up from the newspaper he is reading. "Now wait a minute," he says, taking off his glasses. "What is it you are trying to say? As far as I can see, there is no difference between men and women at all."

"How many men you know got a pussy?" Speed asks.

Doc folds his glasses and puts them in his shirt pocket. He smiles. When the men finish laughing, Doc says, "Now you know that is not what I meant. But since you do not seem to understand, I will break it down for you. What I am saying is that there is no essential difference between men and women. There are just as many men as there are women out there who are not to be trusted."

Jenkins looks at Doc from underneath his green eyeshade. "Doc," he says, "you wrong when you say there ain't no difference. It's a whole lotta men I wouldn't turn my back on. But I'll tell you one thing—a man might dog a woman, but a woman will give a man the blues for life."

"That may be true," Doc says. "But even if it is, none of it is any worse than what black men have always done to black women."

Hubble lowers his clippers and looks over at Jenkins. "All this y'all talking about got me thinking," he says. "Know who I ain't seen in a long time?"

Speed says, "Your daddy?" and a ripple of appreciative laughter runs down the line of waiting men.

Hubble frowns.

"Speed, I done told you," he says. "I do not play that mess. Now come on now, boy—you might get hurt."

"Hurt?" Speed looks sideways at Hubble. "Hurt? Man, you better think twice before you mess with me. I'm the one that whipped lightning's ass and put thunder in jail, drunk all the water out the ocean, and tied a knot in the whale's tail."

Hubble tilts his customer's head.

"Uh huh," he says. "Uh huh."

Prudhomme snickers, and Hubble stands back from his customer, his face a mask of blank disdain. Underneath his blue barber's smock he wears a long-sleeved shirt, the same kind he wears every day, always buttoned at the wrist and the collar no matter how hot it is. For the past twenty-four years, Hubble has worked in a hotel restaurant downtown, first as dishwasher, then cook's assistant, then second cook before, finally, head cook. Two years and three months ago, he became kitchen manager. One night every two weeks and one weekend a month, Hubble is absent from Jenkins's shop—those times are reserved for his service in the National Guard. In a year, Hubble will retire from the guard. Five years after that, he will leave the restaurant. He will collect two pensions and still be young enough to cut hair. If he wishes, he can also take another day job. In the fifteen years that he has worked for Jenkins, Hubble has always been on time and seldom sick. He is a good barber. Because of this, he has Jenkins's respect and his own key to the shop.

"You couldn't park in front today, Omar?" Jenkins says. "I didn't see your car."

"Didn't drive. Man didn't have the car ready when I went to get it yesterday."

"You need a ride? Won't be no trouble to drop you off."

Hubble shakes his head.

"Earline picking it up. She'll come for me after nine."

For a few moments the only sound in the shop is the hum of the clippers and the rattle of the old Coke machine. Then Speed says, "Hey, I didn't mean nothing, awright?" He exchanges glances with Prudhomme. "Awright? 'Cause Hubble, I don't know nothing about your daddy—just ask your momma."

"Well, it seemed peculiar to me," Jenkins says, before the laughter can encourage further impudence from Speed. "'Cause I know you can usually find a place in front of the shop."

"Yeah," Hubble says absently, "that's true," and then, "Carver. That's who I was thinking about. What works down at the post office. He still with that young girl?"

"Carver? Lloyd Carver?" Jenkins looks at Hubble and shakes his head. "Omar, where you been, man? They buried Lloyd Carver two weeks ago Friday."

"You got to be kidding me." Hubble considers it. "Come to think of it, last time I seen him Carver look like he'd been sick. But I didn't think he was doing that bad."

"And I'll tell you something else," Jenkins says. "By the time it was over, if it wasn't for the VA Lloyd Carver woulda been in the street. Yeah, that's right." Sweeping the cloth from Perkin's lap, Jenkins looks to see who is next. Prudhomme rises. Despite his appreciation of Speed's gift for insult and exaggeration, Prudhomme trusts only Jenkins to cut his hair.

"Now, see, that's just what I been saying," Jenkins says, pinning the cloth around Prudhomme's neck and then leveling his clippers at Doc. "That girl had Carver's nose wide enough open to drive a Mack truck through. And all the time she was fattening him, fattening him just like you fatten a hog for slaughter."

Doc smiles. Like the best bartenders and cabdrivers, men whose chosen profession also requires them to come daily into contact with members of the public, Jenkins is both a storyteller and a philosopher. Doc knows this, and so do the rest of the men present. Whether this is part of Jenkins's temperament and has always been, or whether it is something Jenkins has learned in his years behind his chair of white enamel, overseeing the heads of men, boys, and the occasional woman, Doc neither knows nor cares. He, and the rest of the men, have long been connoisseurs of Jenkins's stories and those that are told in his shop.

"Well, I did not know Lloyd Carver," Doc says. "So I guess you will have to tell me what happened."

"Doc," Jenkins says, as he begins to work the comb through Prudhomme's hair, "what that woman did to Lloyd Carver was a shame. Took everything he had and after she was finished, she just stepped over where he was laying and kept on going. But man, she musta had some good stuff, because as soon as he met her Carver start to act like he still in school, and here he a grown man with almost thirty-five years at the post office.

"How it started was Carver met the broad in onea them little joints up on Georgia Avenue. Wasn't too long before he ask her to quit her job and come stay in the house he bought after that old lady passed. Now, it was two things that girl could do, and one of them was cook. Every night Carver come home she got the food on the table, cooked just the way he like it. So when he come home one night and dinner ain't ready and she just sitting there with a long face, Carver know something ain't right. He say, 'What's wrong, darling?' The broad say she want to know do Carver love her.

"Carver say, 'Love you? Of course I love you.' So she say, 'Well, I hope so, because you the only thing I got. And if something was to happen to you, I don't know what I'd do.' Carver say, 'Ain't nothing going to happen to me,' but she keep on, till finally he say, 'Darlin', what you want me to do to set your mind at rest?' And she say, 'Lloyd, honey, would you put your car in my name? That way, if something happen to you, I'd at least have me something to ride around in.' Now Carver had him a Park Avenue didn't have but twenty-eight thousand miles on it. But he just laugh and say, 'Is that all you want, honey? Shoot, I'll do it tomorrow.'

"Few weeks later him and the broad sitting in the living room watching the Redskins and the broad say something, but Carver too busy watching—you remember that game where they kick Dallas's ass? That's how come the broad got mad, 'cause Carver wasn't listening. So she got up and turned off the teevee and run upstairs crying."

Speed says, "Turned off the teevee? Turned off the teevee in the man's own house? Shee-it. I'da kicked the bitch's ass in a minit. A red-hot minit."

Jenkins lifts the clippers from Prudhomme's head and looks over at Speed.

"Yeah," he says, "I believe you would have. But all Lloyd Carver done was go upstairs asking himself what the hell was wrong. Get in the bedroom, the broad say, 'Lloyd, I quit working 'cause you axe me, and now I ain't got nothing of my own. And I coulda gone back and finished school and had me a good job working for the government.' Carver say, 'Baby, you ain't got to worry about no job. I'ma take care of you.' Broad say, 'But we got to face facts. I know we got us a good long time left together, but you ain't gon' be here to take care of me forever. What am I gon' do after you gone?'

"Carver say, 'Whatchu want me to do?' Broad look at him. Broad say, 'I'm gon' need something to get by. Will you go in tomorrow and make over your annuity to me?' Now Lloyd been paying into that policy the whole time he been at the post office, and you know the post office got them a good retirement plan— "

"Wait a minute," Doc says. "Wait just a minute. Do you expect me to believe this story? That a man, a grown man, would sign away his car and his insurance to a woman he met in a nightclub? I'm sorry, but I just cannot believe such a thing would happen."

"You ain't as sorry as Lloyd Carver was, once it was all over," Jenkins says, "and I don't care whether you believe or disbelieve. These are true facts I'm telling you. True facts. The next day Carver went in and changed over his policy. Now, once he did that, you'da thought she'd be real nice to him so she could get the rest of what she wanted. But next time Carver try to get him some, the broad say she feeling sick and ask would he mind sleeping on the couch.

"'Nother few weeks go by and Carver still sleeping on that couch. But what shoulda tipped him off is they been living in that house three, four, maybe five months, and the whole time he ain't never seen her nekkid. Now all of a sudden she wearing these little old shortie nightgowns, leave the bedroom door open and he walk past and she laying there ain't wearing nothing but panties. After a while, Carver start to feel like he gon' go crazy he don't get him some.

"One night, she come downstairs wearing one of them old shortie nightgowns. Come in the living room and say, 'Lloyd, we got some stuff we got to talk about.' Carver say, 'What's on your mind, sugar?' Broad say, 'It's more than thirty years difference between us. Now I know you don't like for me to talk like this, but I got to. You ain't gon' be here for me forever, and it's a mean old world for a woman ain't got no man. You got to do something to make it easier for me if you pass.'

"Carver ain't say nothing for a long time. Then he say, 'Woman—you asked me to put my car in your name. I did it. You asked me to make over my retirement to you. I did that too. What you want me to do for you now?' And the broad, she say, 'Lloyd, it ain't for me. It's for the baby.' Carver say, 'Woman, how come you ain't tell me?' She say, 'I just now found out." The two of them sit there grinning at each other, and then she say, "Now come on upstairs with me, Lloyd. I ain't been as good to you as I should.'

"Afterwards, Carver about to fall asleep, and she say, 'Do it for me, Lloyd. Please.' Carver say, 'Do what?' Broad say, 'Put the house in my name. So me and Lloyd Junior can have us a roof over our heads if you pass.' "

"Goddamn," says Prudhomme, "and he did it?" Speed says, "Shee-it." The laughter that comes then is rueful and mocking all at the same time, a taunt and an elegy that celebrates the recklessness of the late Lloyd Carver and his imprudence in the face of love. Only Speed's laughter is entirely without sympathy. Hubble does not laugh. He frowns, the whiskey sadness heavy on his face. "Shee-it," Speed says again, and Jenkins unpins the cloth from Prudhomme's neck. He snaps it to shake off the hair.

"And then?" Doc says as he approaches the chair. "What happened next?"

"Whatchu mean, 'what happened'?"

"I mean what happened? It didn't just end that way. What happened?"

"Whatchu think happened? Wasn't but a couplea days after he put the house in her name, Carver come home and found two suitcases on the porch. Key didn't work 'cause she'd done had the lock changed. Rung the bell, and she come to the door, didn't even open it. Told him to get his ass off her porch before she call the *po*-lice. And when Carver went to see a lawyer the next day, the man said wasn't a damned thing he could do."

"He brought it on himself," Speed says, "letting the bitch game him like that. First time she asked for something, he shoulda told her, 'I give you a roof to sleep under, and a bed to sleep in. You want anything else, go get you a job.'"

"That's right," Prudhomme says. "It's all a game, and the sooner you learn that, the better. See, it's like that old man was trying to get next to this young girl, promised her a whole lotta stuff if she just give him some pussy. Girl finally gave him some leg and he putting his clothes on and she say, 'Now, Daddy, don't forget all them things you said you was gon' do for me.' And he just buttoned his shirt and said, 'Baby, lemme tell you something—when I'm hard, I'm soft. But when I'm soft, baby, I'm hard.'"

Speed laughs and takes a cigarette, a Kool, from the pack on the counter behind his chair. He lights it.

"You got to be that way," he says, "'cause somea these no-good black bitches they got out here will take a man for everything he got, if he let 'em. And it ain't about color. Somea these high-yella and brownskin gals ain't shit neither." Speed blows a jet of smoke out the side of his mouth. "But I still say a real man wouldn't let nothing like that go down. A real man is gon' take charge, a real man know he stronger than a woman."

"Uh huh," Jenkins says. "Well, I can see you ain't never been married, son," and Prudhomme says, "Doc, what you think?"

"Frankly," Doc says, "I still do not see how a man could be so foolish as your friend to sign away his car, his insurance, and his home." Before Jenkins can speak, Doc says, "Also, I prefer to believe black women are not that greedy, at least no more so than any other women."

"Well, that's a true story," Jenkins says, lowering the clippers. "Lloyd Carver told it to me while I was cutting his hair, down to the VA hospital the week before he died."

The telephone rings. Speed picks it up. A moment later he hangs up and, turning to the counter behind his chair, searches for a new blade for his clippers. Catching sight of himself in the mirror, he leans closer, fingering a blemish on his chin.

"Doc," Jenkins says, "you may have plenty of book learning, but you and Speed might as well be twins because the two of you are still as ignorant about some things as the day you were born. Lloyd Carver just couldn't help himself—that little girl's stuff was too good and her game was just too strong."

"Well," Doc says, when he has finished laughing, "all that may be true. And it may be true that I am ignorant. But there is one significant difference between Speed and me—I respect black women. At least I try to."

Speed turns away from the mirror, one fist on his hip. The ash from his cigarette dribbles onto the front of his smock. "Who don't respect black women? I respect all womens. As long as they respect me."

"All right," Doc says, holding up his hands under the cloth in mock surrender. "But that must be a lot of respect, because we all know you have a lot of women. Mr. Jenkins, for the sake of argument, let us say your story is true. Even so, I still say what happened to your friend is no more than what some black women complain some black men have always done to them. And you could even argue that she deserved some compensation for taking care of him."

Jenkins says, "You believe that shit?"

"I certainly do. I read. You should too, and not just the sports pages. You might learn something. Or watch teevee. Like that talk show in the afternoons."

"Which one? Show got that great big old fat broad?"

"She is not fat. Not anymore."

"Huh. Just wait. You'll see—she gon' put it all back on."

"That may be true," Doc says. "But it is neither here nor there as far as what we are talking about."

Jenkins looks at the clock. It is nine, closing time.

"Say, Omar," Jenkins says, "close the door, before some fool can't read try to come in. And turn off the sign."

Hubble goes to do it. When he comes back, he says, "I been standing here listening, and I got to say it's been a long time since I heard Negroes full of shit as y'all is." He unpins the cloth and dusts the back of his customer's neck with talcum. Sweeping the cloth from his customer's lap, Hubble says, "Speed think Carver shoulda smacked the broad, and I can understand that, 'cause Speed's brains in his dick, if he got any. Jenkins, you think it's all about the woman had a better game than Carver. And you, Doc, you can't understand how a man could let something like that happen. But don't nonea y'all know what the hell you talking about. Y'all ever consider the possibility that Lloyd Carver was in love?"

"Love?" Prudhomme says, before the shop explodes with laughter. "Love? Ain't nobody said nothing about love," and Jenkins says, "Omar, whatchu know about a old man and a young girl? You been married to the same woman thirty-two and a half years. And I know you don't do no running around on the side."

"Ain't got to. I love my wife. And I got what I need right at home."

"Shee-it," says Speed. "Don't lie. You be too tired. Working as many jobs as you got."

The men laugh, but Hubble says nothing. The chairs against the wall are almost empty now; only Prudhomme, Doc, and one or two stragglers are left. Hubble folds his cloth, hangs up clippers and scissors. He discards an empty bottle of hair tonic, tosses towels and the folded cloth in an orange nylon bag to go to the laundry on Monday. He counts the money he has taken in, counts out the share that is due Jenkins, and counts it again before giving it to him. Finished, Hubble takes a pair of clippers and a small wire brush. He sits down in his chair. He sits for a long time cleaning the clippers, brow furrowed and his mouth pursed, as if closing in on something he does not yet know if he wants to say. Finally, Hubble says, "Long as y'all telling stories, I got me one."

"Go on," Jenkins says. "If you think we can understand it," and Hubble says, "It was this man one time loved his wife. Loved her more than he did his momma and his daddy, which is only right, because that's what the Good Book say you supposed to do. Every Friday night this man come home with his money and give it to his baby. She didn't even have to ask.

"Now one day him and his wife decide to get them a little house. He didn't want her working, and the only way they could do it was if he went out and got himself another job. Wasn't like it is now—colored man could only find certain types of work. And times was hard, so hard they was a lot of men couldn't even find one job. But this man found him some work washing dishes at night in a restaurant.

"Every morning he get up and go work his regular job. Get off and go wash them dishes till midnight six days a week. Was a whole lotta times he'd come home at night and his baby be sleeping when he get in. A man shouldn't be outside his house like that, not as much as this man was. See, by him being away from home like that, he wasn't able to take care of business. And it was plenty of other men just waiting to take care of it for him.

"One Friday morning, this man getting ready to leave out the house. His wife say, 'What time you comin' home?' He say regular time. And she say she been thinking—bank they been keeping their money in, she been reading the papers, and the money ain't safe no more. She say, 'I want us to take it out. Monday morning we'll find ourselves a good, safe place to put it.'

"He been working himself like a dog for two, almost three years. Had more than five hundred dollars saved up. He say, 'Sugar, you think it's the right thing? I don't like to think about carrying around that kind of money all day like that.' And his wife, she just throw back her head and laugh, say, 'Big as you is, who gon' mess with you?'

"Come lunch time he take all their money out the bank. Walk around all day with them bills folded over in his pocket. Every once in a while reach in his pocket and touch that money, thinking about how a man could work so hard and so long and still have so little. Come midnight, he finish washing dishes in the restaurant and get on the streetcar, thinking how he just want to get home and put that money someplace safe.

"Man get off the streetcar and start walking. Almost to his house when he hear somebody say, 'There he is!' and three men jump out the alley. It's two big men. One got a knife. And it's a little man got a handkerchief over his face. One carry the knife say, 'I'ma have to cut you, you don't give it up.' Little one say, 'Yeah, we know you got it.' This man I'm talking about don't even stop to think about what he doing—he knock down the man closest to him, kick him. Little one yelling, 'Cut him! Cut him!' and the man with the knife bring it down. Man do like this" —Hubble sets the clippers in his lap and raises his arms to cover his face— "and he don't even feel it when the knife cut him, cut the back of his arms from his wrist to his elbows. All he thinking about is how he gots to keep that money.

"Knife come down one more time and he grab the man's arm. Knife fall out the man's hand and he pick it up, turn on the little one. Hit him across the face, raise the knife. And hear the little man say, 'Naw, naw, don't do it. Don't you know who I is? It's me. It's me—'

"Man pull down the scarf, and you know what? It was his wife. It was his wife."

No one says anything, and for a moment the men in the shop can hear all the sounds from outside—footsteps on the sidewalk, laughter from the corner by the liquor store, the cars idling at the stoplight on the Avenue. Finally, Prudhomme whistles.

"Damn," Speed says, "that's some terrible shit. What he do, Hubble? Kick the bitch's ass and leave her in the street?"

"Naw. It didn't go like that. This man, he just left and went on home. Couldn't think of nowhere else to go. Walked in and she waiting with the *po*-lice. Told 'em he beat her. Judge give him six months."

Jenkins turns the chair so that Doc faces the mirror. Their eyes meet, and then both Doc and Jenkins turn to look at Hubble. Neither says anything. Speed says, "Shee-it," and puts down his clippers, disgusted. "Now that's what I been telling you. Man let a bitch run a game on him like that, he gon' get what he deserves. He shoulda smacked her a few times, let her know who was in control."

Hubble laughs.

"Speed, trying to tell you something is like trying to preach the Bible to a cat. Yeah, this man I'm talking about, he coulda beat her—he was twice her size, but this man, see, he loved that woman. And while he was in jail, the woman searched her heart and come to understand how wrong she'd been. When he got out she came to find him. They been together ever since."

The telephone rings. Speed hesitates, unable to decide. He wants to set Hubble straight, but there is a little girl waiting. In the end he goes to answer the telephone. Jenkins, still looking curiously at Hubble, says, "Omar, long as you been working in my shop, I ain't never heard you tell no story. Least not like that. Now lookahere—"

Before Jenkins can finish, a car horn sounds outside and Hubble goes to the window. He waves, then turns. "Gentlemen," Hubble says, "y'all gon' have to excuse me, but that's my wife."

As the door closes after him, Prudhomme says, "I don't know about y'all, but I don't believe a word..." and then he makes the connection, the same connection Doc and Jenkins have already made.

A man can learn many things in Lamarr Jenkins's shop—what to put into a transmission or a motor to keep a vehicle running long past its time; where to get the freshest fish, the cheapest TV, the best suit; how to slaughter a hog or raise a sagging roof. And, sometimes, what a man learns may remind him of the true facts—that he can work alongside another man for fifteen years, can know him for that time and more, and still not know all there is to know about him. Prudhomme joins Doc and Jenkins at the window.

The big-bodied Chevrolet is double parked. Hubble walks to the driver's side while his wife slides over. There is nothing remarkable about her—she is a plump, brown-skinned woman with graying hair and a sweet, dimpled face. Hubble gets in and puts the Chevrolet in gear. Doc, Prudhomme, and Jenkins stand watching, long after Hubble has driven off.

Leaning against the wall with the telephone against his ear, Speed shifts the cigarette dangling from his lips and squints past the smoke. "Hey," Speed calls, "whatch'all looking at?"

Jenkins turns, motioning for Doc to sit down so that he can finish and they can all go home. "Never mind," Jenkins says. "Never mind. It ain't got a thing to do with you."

FLYING HOME

He knows why he's brought her, but now that they're here in the old neighborhood, on the same familiar street, in front of the very house he grew up in, Shepherd isn't sure what he's supposed to show his daughter. It's been more than seventeen years since the death of the woman he sometimes calls his mother, a slip born of grief become wishful thinking that he almost always catches before he'd have to correct himself. The truth is that Mrs. Pettigrew was only the woman who raised him, which helps to explain why, in the years since her passing, he has quite literally never come back to this street. Old memories are stirring. Shepherd shouldn't be surprised, but he is. And there's something else struggling to claim his attention, the possibility that the decision to come back might not just be about Jessica. That there might be something waiting in ambush because he does not know it's what he's looking for.

Slumped beside him in tennis whites, Jessica looks dubiously at the freshly painted brick house. Behind the fleur-de-lis spikes of the wrought-iron fence, the concrete steps have been bricked over. Spider plants in clay pots hanging from thick yarn ropes behind iron-barred windows provoke Shepherd's wry smile. Mrs. Pettigrew would have said the plants were a sign the Street was coming back: White people had moved in.

Another sign approaches in the mirror—a woman, blond hair pulled back by a green fluorescent band. Lean and long-limbed in shorts and jersey, she slices into the street to bypass two slim brownskin girls turning double-dutch on the sidewalk. A third girl skips deftly inside the flashing arcs, ashy legs flailing beneath a plaid parochial school skirt.

Another waits her turn. The running woman turns at the corner, ignoring catcalls from a knot of men and women passing a bag-covered bottle as they sit perched on a stoop.

Except for the running woman and the house with the spider plants, the Street is just the way Shepherd remembers it.

"This is it?" Jessica says. "This is what you brought me here to see?"

"It's where I grew up. That's the house I—"

"We're not going in, are we?"

There's a hint of a whine in Jessica's voice, and Shepherd shakes his head. He'll go for a run later, he decides, skip dinner and go for a long one, deep into Rock Creek Park before turning for home at dusk, hot and sweaty, legs quivering.

"My mo—" Shepherd halts, catching himself. "Mrs. Pettigrew's been gone for years. I don't know who lives here now."

The face could mean Jessica's disappointed or that she's relieved. It's possible, too, the face has nothing to do with where they've come to, is simply a product of the early-teen mood swings that sour her seemingly at random. Half-in half-out of the BMW's open door, Shepherd stalls, wondering how to continue.

It had seemed necessary, even overdue, watching the gaggle of Cathedral schoolgirls—black, white, Hispanic, Asian—leave the courts on Woodley Road. Jessica and two or three others wore tennis whites. Alyse had been one of a handful of early black students—and the only one not on scholarship—and she insisted on them for their daughter. The rest were dressed alike in jeans or khakis and button-down boy's shirts, a few with earrings and garish, brightly colored plastic costume jewelry. The girls sounded alike too, voices bland and accentless, conversation littered with *For sures* and *I was likes* and *That was so like you knows*. Shepherd tested and found true the theory that raised in him a sudden alarm: Eyes closed, it was impossible to tell them apart.

He found it disturbing, yet was disturbed that he was disturbed, as if he'd been brought face to face with some hypocrisy he'd avoided long enough to believe it no longer mattered. Alyse's mother, Camille, wanted Jessica to join Jack and Jill. She was on the board of the fifty-year-old, invitation-only social club for the children of what passed for a black American aristocracy. She herself had been a member. Alyse had too; Jessica's selection was assured. But to what end? Camille's parents—and, in turn, Camille herself—had found it necessary to protect their children from a segregated world; why was it necessary to protect Jessica from an integrated one?

"I forgot—," Shepherd says, asking it now as he turns to look at the daughter who sometimes seems almost a stranger to him, "—how was tennis?"

"Okay."

"Just okay?"

"I'm not sure I want to keep taking lessons."

"You don't have to. But it'd be nice if you kept doing a sport. What about basketball?"

"Basketball?" Jessica rolls her eyes and tightens her lips as if the word leaves a bad taste. "Because that's what black kids do?"

"Black kids?" Shepherd sputters, and Jessica says with sweet reasonableness, "We're not all alike. But I can't help it if some people can't tell there's differences."

Shepherd stands, unfolding himself into the street. Some people? Other girls, teachers at school? Himself? He should have ready a response, but what?

"Come on," he says. "I want to show you something."

Jessica pushes herself out, loosing a barely suppressed sigh. Glancing at the backseat—there is only a small maroon

Olsson's bag resting precariously atop a litter of academic papers and journals; nothing worth stealing—Shepherd thumbs the remote to lock the doors. The girls stop to switch off, clothes-line jump rope limp in their hands, allowing them to pass. Once they're by, the girls start again, chanting in unison:

Wish I had a nickel,
Wish I had a dime,
Wish I had a sweetheart.
Love me all the time.
Make him wash the dishes,
Make him scrub the floor,
And when he get finished,
I'd kick him out the door!

He wants Jessica to ask if she can try. Surely the girls won't mind. Jessica's agile enough to pick it up easily, but boredom's plain in her sullen listlessness. Shepherd turns back as the girl inside the whirling ropes skips out and another slips smoothly in. They begin a new chant:

Charlie Chaplin went to France,
Teach those girls the hula-hula dance...

Did they sing that same rhyme? Not these girls, but their mothers and grandmothers, the girls he knew when he was a boy. Shepherd thinks so, and he wonders how the rhymes get passed down and whether Charlie Chaplin is more than a name to these girls. He's a curator at the Smithsonian, would brood about provenance and variation, classify and categorize even if he weren't paid to. Abstraction, Alyse chides, is his way of avoiding emotion, and it's true now—though it isn't just idle curiosity, it's also a way to avoid engaging Jessica's mood.

At the end of the block, the Street spills into Anna J. Cooper Circle. Ahead is the house where Robert and Mary Church Terrell lived. Farther on to the northwest, but still easy walking distance, is Howard University. The area is redolent with history—Langston Hughes lived nearby during a Washington sojourn, though Shepherd isn't sure where. His own history suffuses him now, giddying him with nostalgia: The alleys where he played basketball before he graduated to the playground, the smell of chalk dust and the blackwash staining his hands after he stayed late to help the teacher clean the chalkboards. The walk home scanning the sidewalk for soda bottles to trade for penny candy at the corner store kept by the Chinese family that lived upstairs above it.

Shepherd thinks about telling Jessica all this, but the set of her shoulders and her clenched jaw remind him she doesn't yet believe, not truly, not yet, that there was a time before her, and so she cares no more about history (even his own) than he did when he, too, was fourteen.

"All right," he says, responding to her unspoken protest. They've only come a few hundred feet, but going on isn't worth what it will surely cost. And, besides, there's his run later, a good, long one, seven miles, perhaps even ten. "We can go back now."

Some apprehension, the rustling of long-dormant skills that once preserved him on these streets, causes Shepherd to look up. Beyond the girls skipping rope, a woman in baggy jeans and sweatshirt struggles up from the stoop at the end of the block. Loosing a braying laugh, she stumbles as she avoids a grasping hand and turns to weave her shambling way up the sidewalk. Shepherd squints watching her, remarking something half-familiar in the way she carries herself.

"Get the fuck out the way," she says loudly to the girls. "Y'all don't own the gat-dam sidewalk."

"You don't own it either," retorts one girl turning rope, and the girl in the plaid skirt says, "Oooh, you curse. I'ma tell my momma."

The woman throws back her head and brays again, her laughter derisive and affectionate. It's laughter of a kind Shepherd has not often heard since abandoning the Street.

Smoothing the dirt-streaked sweatshirt over her distended stomach, the woman eyes him as she approaches. It's a pathetic attempt to make herself presentable. There's a picture of Lucy on the shirt, Lucy from "Peanuts" in brown face, her mouth twisted in the familiar crabby sneer, puffy Afro instead of the comic strip character's dense bun.

"He'p me out?" the woman says, and Jessica flinches at the grimace of missing teeth meant for a smile. Her face is ashen and puffy, one eye swollen shut by a blue-black bruise, the yellow sclera of the other streaked with red veins. A half-smoked cigarette is tucked into a tangle of matted hair.

"C'mon," she pleads, abject aggressiveness beyond shame. "I need me some carfare go to the hospital."

Jessica stares, repulsed and fascinated. "It's okay," Shepherd murmurs. Reaching into his pocket, he finds a fistful of change, pours it into the woman's waiting palm without looking to see how much it is.

She takes it without thanks, accepting the money as matter-of-factly as if Shepherd were settling a debt. Cocking her head, she fixes him with her good eye before she moves on, shambling and splay-footed.

Shepherd is beside the BMW, thumbing the remote to open the door for Jessica, when he hears the call:

"Hey, hol' on nigger—don't I know you?"

Jessica's eyes go wide. She looks down the street and then up at her father, willing him to deny it. Shepherd wants to but he can't—he sees who it is now behind the ravaged face, sees it as clearly as if a breeze had lifted a curtain and thrown light into a dim room. Marvella Whitman. In high school she'd been the kind of plump they called "phat" (and which college taught him to call *zaftig*), fast and eager with soft, butter-colored skin. He conjures the feel of her body against his in some dim memory-summoned basement lit by blue bulbs; half-high on coarse red wine and slow-dragging to Smokey Robinson crooning "Oooh-oooh-oooh, baby, baby." Shepherd quickens. Marvella broke his heart with her rude vitality; now the evidence of her destruction threatens to break it again.

"Damn," Marvella says. "I know I know you, nigger. Sherm, right? Naw, that ain't it. Sh— Sh—"

"Shepherd," he says, even as Marvella remembers and says it with him, "Shepherd. Yeah, thass right. Shepherd."

He smiles despite his horror at what survives of her, and Marvella returns the smile, the ghost of the sweet girl haunting her face before it disappears again. Above the image of sepia Lucy on her sweatshirt are the words "I Love Black People." And, beneath, "It's Niggers I Can't Stand."

"Marvella," Shepherd says. "How're you doing? It's been a long time."

"Shee-it—" Marvella grimaces at Jessica, bobs her head in half-apology. "'Scuse me, I ain't mean no disrespect but damn, you got eyes." She gestures, taking in the BMW with its leather seats and Blaupunkt stereo, Shepherd in his tan corduroy jacket and gleaming loafers. "Wish I's doing good as you. Damn, nigger, I thought you was dead. Or in jail, like them crazy muthafuckers you always be running with."

Shepherd laughs uneasily, and Jessica opens the door and gets in. She straps herself behind the seatbelt and pulls the door closed against Marvella's ruined glory.

Leaning towards the car, Marvella grins her gap-toothed grimace. "Don't be 'fraida me," she says to her reflection in the window. "I been used hard and I look it. But you ain't gotta be 'fraid."

Jessica shrinks as if Marvella could touch her, and Marvella straightens out of her disappointment. She moves towards Shepherd, close enough for him to smell stale sweat and sour wine. She grins, willfully summoning optimism.

"Damn, but you lookin' prosperous, Shep."

"Yeah? How you know I ain't frontin'?" Shepherd says, slipping easily into the vernacular, the common tongue of street corner, beauty- and barbershop, voice becoming softer, more Southern, consonants losing their edges.

"Huh! You fronting, you still doing better than me. C'mon—lemme hol' on a couplea dollars 'fore you go."

Shepherd laughs and shrugs, displaying empty hands.

"C'mon," Marvella says. "I know you got it." And then, when he makes no move for his wallet, "Least lemme ride witchu. I been supposed to be at the clinic up on U Street, and you know I can't catch no cab with this little piecea change."

"Where on U?" Shepherd asks, and Jessica straightens, looking incredulously at her father through the glass. The irritation that has been chafing him since he met her at school begins to heat into anger, and he realizes he wants her to feel something, anything, besides disdain. There's another world beyond the one she knows of Chevy Chase, the Cathedral schools, and play dates negotiated as carefully as business treaties. Alyse would prefer she know nothing of that other world, wants to shield her from it. He understands. Yet how to teach his daughter she doesn't have to want that world, but doesn't have to fear or despise it either?

Even as he thinks this, Shepherd's anger turns away from the daughter he loves all the more because she's slipping away from him. What right does Marvella, wasted and shambling, have to ask even this small favor? The choices that have left her this way are her own and not of his making. Still, he knows he cannot refuse. The same survivor's guilt that fuels his anger also compels him to take her.

Jessica coughs, wrinkling her nose at the acrid odor of urine that invades the car as Marvella lurches wheezing into the back. Marvella twists to tug at the seatbelt, knocking aside the welter of papers and the Olsson's bag, spilling journals, abstracts, and the copy of Chesnutt's *The Wife of His Youth and Other Stories* that Shepherd had bought at lunch.

"Daddy," Jessica says, one hand daintily over her face. "Daddy."

"It's on the way," he says, turning the key in the ignition before he presses the switch to roll down the windows. It isn't, but he pretends certainty; it's easier than explaining why he must do this. "We'll be home soon."

From the back, Marvella says, "What you do you can afford this kinda car? Work for the government?"

"Kind of. I'm at the Smithsonian."

"No shit? One with the elephant?"

Shepherd's surprised. And then he remembers the field trips she looked forward to because they meant getting out of school.

"That's Natural History," he says. "I'm at American. The one with the flag."

"Damn! I always knew you had it in you. Probably got some white folks working for you. Now I know you doing good."

Past the circle, as he's about to turn onto Florida Avenue, the light turns red and Shepherd brakes, a few yards from the corner and Kim's Carryout, Chinese and American Food, Chicken Wings with Mumbo Sauce. Music thuds from a double-parked car, adolescent vulgarities and empty boasts overwhelming the drive-time jazz, WPFW, Shepherd has on the radio:

Simple muthafukkas don't know how to get their grind on
Dont fukk wid the baddest mutha love to get his freak on
Never wanna hurt love if love ain't puttin' a show on
Born and raised a thug, Huh!
And I'ma trust in God long as he let me play on.

A plague of drug boys lounge by the carryout before ornate spray-painted graffiti—hard-eyed teenagers in baggy jeans and basketball shoes, bandanas and t-shirt kaffiyeh wrapped round their heads. One scans the cars for customers. Two others keep watch for police.

"Hey!" Marvella screeches out the window. Jessica cringes. "You—Antuan! How many times I tol' you to keep your black ass off this corner?"

One of the lookouts cuts his eyes towards the BMW. He's wearing the same uniform of baggy jeans and basketball shoes with the laces untied, t-shirt billowing almost to his knees. He could be sixteen or twenty. Another boy laughs, says, "Go on home, nigga. Yo' momma's callin'."

"Dantae, shut up," Marvella shouts. "Ain't nobody talking to you. 'Tuan, you better get off this corner 'fo' I come out this car and put foot in your narrow ass."

"Marvella," Shepherd says.

"He ain't slinging rock." Her fierce voice dares Shepherd to contradict her, though she's fixed on 'Tuan as he slinks off the corner. Far enough away to make it clear he's left only because he wants to, he begins to run, fists pumping, long legs carrying him swiftly away. Still watching, Marvella says, "Ain't gon' stand for that. But he don't understand—bullet don't give a damn if you slingin' or just chillin' with your friends."

Jessica sits rigidly, hands clasped as if she's praying, though Shepherd thinks he detects something else besides fear on her face—a kind of chary fascination, as if one of her friends had talked her into a horror movie her parents insisted she's not ready for and she's determined to keep watching to prove them wrong. The light changes, and Shepherd eases the BMW forward.

"Damn it's good to see you," Marvella says. "Don't nobody come 'round no more. Ain't seen Wallace since Miz Renfro died. You remember Wallace? Him and his brother Wilson?"

"Wilson used to go with P.J.'s sister, Charlene? No, wait, that was Wallace. All y'all girls liked Wallace 'cause he could rap so good."

"Dance, too. Work for the gas company. His brother drive for Metro. They in the county, so you know they doing good. Rest of 'em—" Marvella shakes her head. "They all fu— They all messed up. P.J.—ol' light-skin pretty P.J.—he doin' five to twelve down Lorton." She laughs, a malicious jeer. "Say he went in a tight end, now he a wide receiver. And Charlene, you wouldn't recognize her, she been on the pipe so long. Her mother keeping the kids."

Marvella pauses, fingering her swollen eye. She winces and touches it again gingerly, then takes the cigarette from behind her ear, puts it between bruised lips. "Marvella," Shepherd says. Muttering "Shee-it," Marvella replaces the cigarette behind her ear and sits back.

"What about 'Vise?" she says. "Y'all used to so be tight. Everybody always figure y'all'd hook up and live happily ever after. Then you went away to college and she just dropped outta sight." Marvella looks cannily at Shepherd, as if there's more and they both know it, but she wants to hear him say.

"Altovise's in North Carolina," Shepherd says. "At least that's what somebody at a conference told me. That was a while ago."

"What she doin' down there?"

"I think they said she's teaching."

"*'Vise?* Teachin' school?"

"College. She's a professor."

"Damn! Girl useta hook school more than I did. That's good money, right? Tell her I said hi, you ever talk to her. You hear from anybody else?"

"Not really."

"I ain't surprised. You pulled a lot of fucked-up shit, but I always knew you wasn't like everybody else. You and 'Vise did what the rest of us need to do—get the hell out the ghetto."

Jessica shoots Shepherd a quick, curious glance that Shepherd pretends not to see. Before he can admonish Marvella about her language, she begins again, listing names Shepherd only half-remembers. She knows what's happened to everyone. The ones who aren't dead or in prison, lost to crime or drugs, live in Prince George's—"the county"—work as secretaries and bank tellers, drive buses or subway trains, read meters for the gas company, run lines for Pepco. A few who'd finished D.C. Teachers or U.D.C. teach school or work for the government.

Shepherd looks out, half-listening as he nods with feigned interest at the dismal litany. That would have been his life, he thinks. That would have been his life, if he'd stayed.

outside the bmw, U Street is a patchwork of new storefronts and boarded-up buildings. It's been years since the riots that left the storefronts smashed and the street littered with broken glass, long enough for Mrs. Pettigrew to be proven right: White people, drawn by cheap rent and the promise of a new subway station, have returned to the city. Many of the old brick buildings that lined the street have been torn down for the Metro, leaving vacant lots strewn with rubble. Here and there, surviving nineteenth-century rowhouses have been restored. The newness of the historically accurate colors makes them look like relics or artifacts. Men in hard hats swarm over other buildings, the brick fronts scrubbed unnaturally pink, like dermabraded skin. The material used to remove the paint is called Peel Away.

Once there was everything here that black men and women in (and striving to become of) the city used to make their own world—banks, stores, nightclubs, restaurants, movie theaters. All are gone now, torn down or boarded up, except the Lincoln and Howard theaters there is talk of renovating. Gone, too, are the doctors and dentists, the real estate, insurance, and burial society agents, the funeral homes, the tailors and seamstresses, the bowling alley, drugstores, and five-and-dimes that made this street the heart of colored Washington. Looking out the window, Shepherd nods at something Marvella is saying, desolate at the betrayal of the past, a kind of treason or blasphemy. Gone, all gone, except for traces like the half-circle of lights over the Ben's Chili Bowl sign next to the Lincoln. The building was once a movie theater, one of the city's first.

"Pull over," Marvella rasps. "Right here. You ain't gotta park."

Shepherd finds a space anyway, waits as Marvella opens her door. But she does not leave, only remains looking at him as if reluctant to take the first step or as if there is something more she needs.

"Supposed to come yesterday," she says finally, "see if a bed opened up. Gon' get myself together. Swear to God, Shep. I'ma do it this time."

He nods and then, because it is not enough, says, "I know. I know you will," and unbuckling his shoulder harness turns to reach over the seat, scraping against the headliner as he pulls her awkwardly towards him. Jessica shrinks away as he squeezes Marvella close despite the smell of sweat, wine, and urine.

A saccharin ballad from some passing car floats through the window, a boy-man's naked wail that isn't about love or sex but the desperate longing for completion. It's as desperate as the yearning for Heaven in the spirituals, a longing so ingrained it might be racial, born out of being strangers in a strange land. Perhaps the song—and all the rest like it in the ever-changing but always the same seasons of pop music—is a code. Music's always contained secrets that could get you killed—the location of a camp meeting; the time of the runaways' departure. Songs like this one can lead you to court the wrong man's woman and die violently; lead you to love the wrong woman and die slowly. Because it really is possible—though who still thinks so anymore?—to die of a broken heart if you're fool enough to take as gospel all the song promises.

The song passes, leaving Shepherd's useless hunger for home mired in its wake. Still holding Marvella, he breathes another scent beneath the wine and her sweat—or is it only his imagination?—a scent faded and sweet, cheap but vital, like the long-gone ghosts of U Street. Marvella's body is slack but still lush, still ripe beneath the stained sweatshirt. It's another long-gone ghost, this feeling he once had for her that's mostly pity now.

Releasing her, Shepherd turns away, blinking back tears. Marvella steps out and slams the door closed, leans into Jessica's open window grinning happily, a ghost Shepherd wishes he could summon back forever, the girl who wore short skirts and black fishnet stockings to school, white brassiere glowing beneath a sheer black blouse, and dared the principal to speak.

"Damn, Shep," she says. "It was good to see you. Nigger just disappear like you did, you don't know if he dead or just said fuck the ghetto."

"Maybe it's the same thing sometimes," Shepherd says, and Marvella laughs, puzzlement beneath the sharp, unpleasant bark. Jessica studies her father, eyes appraising.

Where did the words come from? Shepherd wonders. And what do they mean? Marvella shambles towards the gap between cars, steps off into the gutter, and stands waiting for a lull in the onrush of traffic. Shepherd watches, wondering if she'll really do it this time. This was how it was for his mother, he understands—though in truth he knows only a little of the story—his real mother of whom nothing remains except constructs, memories of memories. She fought, but she was weak, and so she fell.

Shepherd opens the door and steps out into the street, reaching for his wallet. He takes out two twenties, a ten, a five, and several wrinkled ones, all the money he's carrying.

"Hey," he calls, holding out his hand, folded-over bills concealed as if offering a tip. "You might need this. For cigarettes. Or candy."

"I knew you had it," Marvella crows as she tucks the wedge into a pocket of her dirt-streaked jeans. "I knew you had it."

"well," jessica says when he gets back into the car. "That was interesting."

"I'm sorry," he says. "That's not what I wanted you to—I had no idea Marvella was going to be..."

Jessica makes a strangled sound, a cough or a sob, sniffing and wiping her eyes. She's crying, Shepherd thinks, a delayed reaction to the stress. He feels oddly satisfied, and is immediately ashamed. Still, he can't deny to himself that he wanted her to feel something, anything.

"I'm sorry," Shepherd says again. "If I'd known, I wouldn't have brought you. But maybe it's not such a bad thing for you to have seen her. That could have been me. Things weren't all that different for us growing up."

Jessica reaches for the glovebox. She takes out a package of tissues, splits the plastic wrap, and blows her nose with a rude, unladylike honk.

"Allergies," she says, and blows her nose again. "I forgot to take my pill."

Shepherd nods and Jessica looks at him, her gaze intense, assessing, as if she's trying to decide whether what she wants is worth the risk.

"If I ask you something," she says, "will you tell me?"

"If I can," Shepherd says.

But he knows what she wants and so, when she does not go on, says, "Sweetheart," touching her gently to lessen the sting of what he must teach her. "Not everybody has what we have. Not everybody's that fortunate. Some people start off with a lot less. A lot less. And the thing is, you just can't—"

"You think I don't know that?" Jessica says, meeting his gaze defiantly. "That's not what I wanted to know."

"What is it then?"

"What happened? Tell me what happened."

"I don't know," Shepherd replies. "Marvella and I haven't seen each other in twenty years. That's a long—"

"Not her," Jessica says. "You. Why didn't you turn out like that if the two of you weren't so different?"

The question cuts to the heart of things, but how to answer? Tell her Marvella grew up poor and deprived, abandoned by her parents, taken in by a woman who cared less about caring for her than the monthly check from the city? It wasn't true, not for Marvella. Her mother was a secretary; her father drove a city trash truck. What about history, then, the dismal stories of crime and recrimination, despair and deprivation, the centuries of familiar, heartbreaking grievances? They were all true, all real, but where to stop? You could go all the way past slavery and the Middle Passage and deep into the lost African past without finding answers.

Because none of it really explains what happened, how it is he isn't dead or in prison, doesn't drive a bus or swab floors to eke out a living, doesn't slump home at night to gape bleary-eyed at everything the television offers that can never be his.

"I was lucky," he says slowly. "I liked books and I liked school and I didn't care some people thought that was acting white. There were teachers at school—and some people at church—who saw something in me before I was ready to see it in myself."

Shepherd pauses, hoping it is enough.

"Mostly, though, I guess I was just lucky," he finishes.

None of what he's just told her is untrue, but it's unsatisfying, no more revealing or insightful than the easy banalities: Everyone makes his own life. People get what they deserve. It's just who you are and what you choose. The truth, one he knows Jessica's not ready to hear, is that he made himself up as he went along without too much thinking about it. It really was luck that brought him to this place now, this moment here past the questions he had (and still has) no answers for. Because if he'd stopped for the questions—How did you live a life that nothing in the experience of anyone you knew prepared you for? Where did you go for direction? Who did you consult about which parts of your old life, your history, your past, to discard and which to take with you?—he might never have gotten started.

The bagpipe plaint of John Coltrane's soprano sax comes from the radio—"My Favorite Things"—and Shepherd blinks back tears as he looks away from his daughter's searching eyes. Through the music and the damp film, he sees the street for an instant as it is and as it was, the past underlying the present, obscured by only the thinnest of veils. It's like discovering he can see ghosts, can summon sounds long since faded into silence. If he gives it all his attention, he can almost hear Duke Ellington's Washingtonians in the elegant ballroom of the Whitelaw Hotel, Billy Eckstine's big band at the Lincoln Colonnade, Coltrane's world-weary sax at the Bohemian Caverns, Lionel Hampton at the Howard the night he and his band blew so strong they convinced a hophead in the balcony he could fly. And Shepherd has only to look slant to see the thoroughfare bustling with actors and musicians, the Grays in town for a doubleheader at Griffith Stadium, Pullman porters about to take off on a West Coast run hailing a cab for Union Station, women in bright red lipstick sashaying on the sidewalk, hair freshly straightened, summer frocks shimmering in the summer twilight. It's Thursday, maid's night out.

Sighing, Shepherd wipes dry eyes with the back of his hand, stifling the urge to wail, to mourn. He's a curator, and so he, at least, continues to keep faith with the past. He finds small comfort in that knowledge. Once it was enough, and it will be again. It has to be.

But now he wants only to get away, if only for a while. He imagines himself on the run he craves, alone, isolate, leaping long strides across a field, beating his arms winglike. A hop, a skip, the surprise of soaring. As soon as he realizes he's flying, he falls. Outstretched arms struggling for purchase, he ignores the disappointment that cripples him to earth. And then, as if in a dream where he becomes what he'd once thought impossible (but will already have forgotten when he awakes), he is aloft.

And perseveres in his element, flying home towards the new life that awaits him.

Turning back to Jessica, he understands she knows he went away and has come back again. The hint of irony in her assessing gaze tells him that. It's the way Alyse sometimes regards him. Jessica's adopted that same gaze, or perhaps it's part of the inheritance none of them has ever given a thought to. Which makes Jessica, in some profound sense, more Alyse's than his. But it doesn't mean there isn't still time, doesn't mean that time won't one day bring her understanding of everything he himself has only accepted.

Shepherd reaches to turn the key. Soon they'll be speeding up Rock Creek Parkway through the oasis of green that stretches from the tip of Washington south to Georgetown, splitting the northern half of the city into black and white.

In a little while, he'll go running.

And then, all at once, so quickly it stabs him with surprise, Jessica's ironic facade crumples and she begins to cry, wracking sobs that shake the shoulders that are all Shepherd can see of her because she's shuttered her face in her hands. He puts his arm around her and pulls her close, holds her for a long time, the ghosts of the street forgotten, strokes her hair and soothes her with wordless murmurs.

Jessica draws away, her face sullen and vulnerable all at the same time in a way that melts Shepherd's heart. Bereft of understanding, he takes a tissue to wipe her face.

"Don't cry," he says. "We're done here. Let's go home now."

Lower lip quivering, eyes still flowing, Jessica wails, "Oh, God, you can't see it, can you? That's not why I'm crying. I'm crying because you can't."

SAVING JIMI HENDRIX

(SLIGHT RETURN)

This is how I save Jimi Hendrix's life:

He's sitting on the balcony, looking out over downtown Washington, waiting for the first rays of the new rising sun. It's dark enough so I can just make out the halo of his Afro. As I come closer, I see he's shirtless, a gold chain around his neck. He's wearing a pair of striped bell-bottoms.

"Hey," I say.

Jimi looks at me and then away again. He looks wistful, vulnerable, nothing like the crazed nigger juju man who tore up the stage at the Ambassador last night.

"Hey," he says warily.

We're in one of those old mansions in Kalorama, a faded Beaux-Arts grande dame, the balcony looking down towards what people who visit from other places think is Washington—the Capitol and the distant white icons of the monuments.

Behind us, the living room (as big as a basketball court) is littered with bodies, people curled up on the floor, slumped on the sofa, Frye boots and bare feet on the coffee table. The ashtrays overflow with cigarette butts and roaches. It's a pharmaceutical buffet, Baggies of pot and pills everywhere; crystal bowls filled with uppers and downers; coke and mescaline in silver gravy boats; slim brass opium pipes and balls of black, tarry opium.

I can hear Country Joe and the Fish on a record player inside, that dirge from *Electric Music for the Mind and Body*, the first album, where he calls for the reefer to be passed, swearing this time he'll get high enough to never have to come down.

Now, on the balcony with Jimi, the world smeared at the edges, colors too bright and oversaturated, as if I was watching a movie, I realize you can get that high, but it doesn't matter—sooner or later, you'll come down anyway.

Which is what I want to tell Jimi.

"Look," I begin, and he turns towards me, frowning as if he'd been writing lyrics in his head and I've made him lose one.

"You've got to change your life," I say. "You have to."

Jimi looks at me quizzically, and then his face changes, becoming tolerant with condescension, as if I'm just another stoned teeny-bopper, another fan who hasn't figured out that all you can really take away is the music; the rest is private.

"I'm not fucked up," I say. "At least not so it matters. You've got three years left. Three years, then you're going to die. You'll take some pills in London. You'd been having trouble sleeping."

Jimi laughs.

"How the hell you know, man?"

How do I know it? It's tempting to say I come from the future, and it seems almost true. But of course it can't be. There was just a lot of good shit last night, that's all, enough to give me a glimpse of the future and myself as a fifty-five-year-old man. Maybe, I think, if I can save Jimi, I can save myself.

"I know it," I say. "I don't know how, but I do."

"Yeah?"

Jimi looks almost interested, as if I'm a distraction from whatever brought him out to the balcony, made him forsake the booze and the drugs and the girls who want to be able to tell their friends they fucked Jimi Hendrix last night.

"What else you know?"

I tell him, as much as I remember from the haze of the night's excesses—Woodstock, the Experience's final breakup, the Band of Gypsies with Billy Cox and Buddy Miles, the shitty contracts and the ghouls fighting for a piece of him, how, Gil Evans and Miles Davis will want to record with him but it will be too late.

His eyes widen at Miles's name, but what he really wants to know is how I know about Billy Cox.

"You in the Army? You Airborne?"

"No," I start, and then from behind us I hear someone call, "Jimi, Jimi?"

She's a little blonde posing in the open French doors, all soft curves and pouty lips, naked under a gaudy Indian print bedspread.

"Where'd you go?" she says, voice a sleepy whine. She blinks in the gathering dawn. "It's so early."

Jimi gets up and walks over to her, reaches inside the bedspread to cup one of her breasts. It's stiff-nippled and perfect, small enough to fit inside a teacup. Before they go back inside, he turns to me and says, "Stick around. I want to hear some more that shit."

"All right," I say, and I turn back to watch the sun rise, smiling to myself and thinking how I may just have saved Jimi Hendrix's life.

it didn't happen that way, of course, though I did see Jimi Hendrix in Washington that August of 1967. I was sixteen, working a summer job in a city office pulling blueprints for city inspectors, architects, and contractors while I waited for the summer to be over and my last year of high school to start. Afterwards, I'd go home, shower, and lie on my bed in the sweltering Washington heat with my head between the speakers of the cheap stereo my mother had ordered years before from the Columbia Record Club. I'd listen to the Beatles, the Stones, or the forty-five of Bob Dylan's "Like a Rolling Stone," wondering when I'd finally be able to score some pot so I could find out what Dylan was really talking about.

On one of those evenings, my best friend Andy called and asked if I wanted to see Hendrix the next night. Hendrix was going to be playing at the Ambassador, an old movie theater some hippie entrepreneurs wanted to turn into Washington's Fillmore. They'd torn out the seats, painted the walls DayGlo colors, installed light-show paraphernalia.

I said yes, though I'd never heard of Hendrix—none of the Washington stations played him. Andy suggested I wait till later that night and tune my radio to WBZ in Boston.

I didn't know what to make of it when "The Wind Cries Mary" came tinnily—and intermittently—from the speaker of my transistor about midnight. And I didn't know what to make of it the next day when I came home after work with a copy of *Are You Experienced?* from Record City and put it on stereo.

I got it a few hours later when Hendrix, Noel Redding, and Mitch Mitchell strode onto the stage of the Ambassador, long and lean in bell-bottom trousers and florid shirts, two white Hucks and Nigger Jimi. Hendrix and Redding plugged in and, as the first squall of feedback erupted from the towering stack of Marshalls behind them, everyone knew we were headed for the territory.

Andy and Brint—he was a great guitar player, working on a certain local reputation that had just been destroyed—and I looked at each other, the same thought flashing through our heads. We would have given anything to be stoned out of our skulls.

Years later, I learned why Hendrix had come to Washington. His managers had booked the Experience as the opening act of the Monkees tour that July. God, I wish I could have been at one of those concerts! I'd love to have seen the looks on the faces of the mothers and fathers who'd brought their children for the innocent shenanigans of the made-for-TV Monkees the first time Hendrix jammed his Stratocaster between his legs and humped it phallus-like at their prepubescent daughters. ("Daddy, why is that man putting his guitar between his legs like that?") And then, afterwards, at the close of his set, when Hendrix destroyed his amplifiers and set the Strat on fire...

It must have hit those good (white) Americans the same way Little Richard's frenzy, Chuck Berry's duck walk, and Jerry Lee Lewis's antics (bumping the grand piano across stage with his redneck behind) had served notice that there was something coming, and you'd better get with it, or get out of the way.

Hendrix's managers' seemingly counterintuitive move turned out to be a stroke of genius. So many parents complained that the promoters booted the Experience off the tour barely a week after the group had joined it. And the publicity—you can't buy ink like that. Hendrix's managers quickly arranged a series of pick-up gigs in July and August, among them the five-day stint at the Ambassador.

The first night there were a handful of us, so few that after he'd finished his first set Hendrix hung out in the lobby. (I went up and told him how much I liked his music. He said, "Thank you.") There were a hundred or more the second night, but things were still loose enough for the trio to lope across the street to a small club where Earl "Fatha" Hines was playing. They had big grins on their faces, as if they were on top of the world. By Saturday, the next-to-last night, the Ambassador was packed.

Time and a certain immoderate consumption of psychotropic substances in my youth have obscured the details of the performances. I don't remember, for example, what songs Hendrix played. I suspect, though, and a CD of a live performance recorded a month later in Stockholm confirms it, that most came from his first album, *Are You Experienced?*

I remember "Purple Haze," and Hendrix pointing at Noel Redding as he sang, "Excuse me while I kiss the sky," because it sounded like he was saying, "kiss this guy." And introducing "I Don't Live Today." But there must have been a lot of filler or jamming on the blues—or else they played the same songs over and over—because while there was an opening band (the long-forgotten Natty Bumpo), Hendrix and the Experience played at least three sets, forty minutes on, twenty minutes off, as if it were a nightclub.

And of course he did it all, playing the Stratocaster behind his head and with his teeth, thrusting it between his legs. He must have learned those tricks (some, anyway) in his years with Little Richard and the Isley Brothers on the chitlin' circuit. Certainly, they derived from T-Bone Walker's splits and behind-the-head guitar playing and Chuck Berry's duck walk. But if Walker was a prop plane, and Berry a jet, Hendrix was an interstellar rocket blasting its way through known space.

if you'd asked me, in 1967, what seeing Hendrix at the Ambassador meant, I might have laughed and said I wanted to grow up to be him. But if I thought about it a little, I might have said Hendrix gave me a place to stand in the world when he made it cool to be black and like rock music. (He also made it easier to score with white chicks, but that's another subject for another time.)

For a black kid going to a mostly white private school in Washington, D.C., in 1967, that was no small thing. I wasn't part of the first group of black students at Sidwell Friends, just the second. And while we weren't greeted with the kind of hostility the Little Rock Nine faced, being one of a handful put me in an ambiguous (though not always untenable) position.

In the morning, I rode a D.C. Transit bus to school, accompanied by scores of older black women, maids, and domestic workers in neighborhoods like Georgetown, Cleveland Park, and Spring Valley. At dinner at friends' houses after school, we were sometimes served by women who might have been on that same bus in the morning and who were always introduced by their first names. Afterwards, I'd make the reverse journey home, passing from one world to the other and feeling comfortable in neither.

Music was a powerful symbol of that discomfort.

In the 1950s, so I've read, black groups would play Southern dancehalls where blacks and whites were separated by a rope running the length of the dance floor. Sometimes, though, in their enthusiasm, the dancers would bring down the rope, and everyone, black and white, would enjoy the forbidden pleasure of dancing together before the sheriff came.

Even if those stories aren't literally true, they illustrate a larger truth: Rock is the fusion of two cultures. Chuck Berry came to Chess Studios in Chicago wanting to play the blues ("That was our music," his piano player, Johnny Johnson, said), and wound up recording the hit "Maybellene," which was based on Bob Wills's "Ida Red." And while Elvis wanted to sing country, it wasn't until he and his boys were fooling around with bluesman Arthur "Big Boy" Crudup's "That's All Right" in Sam Phillips's Memphis studio that Phillips found what he'd been looking for: "A white boy who could sing with that real Negro feeling." (Whether Elvis's feeling really was "real Negro" is arguable; still, let's give the boy credit for trying.)

By 1967, though, music (for black people at least) had become a racial litmus test, in a way it didn't for whites till the heavy metal era. The betrayal of rock's interracial promise came, not coincidentally, as the hope of the Civil Rights Movement was supplanted by the nihilism of Black Power and the Black Panther Party.

The interesting thing for me was that while the black kids on the Street I grew up on despised the Beatles and the Rolling Stones, the white kids I came to know at Friends were genuinely interested in black music, listening to what their grandparents might have called race music on WOL and WOOK, and venturing down to the Howard Theater (Washington's Apollo) Friday and Saturday nights.

That white fascination with things black dates all the way back to the first Europeans' encounter with Africans on Africa's shores. Still, the length (and complicated nature) of that fascination shouldn't obscure my friends' genuine appreciation of and affection for black music. Certainly that was true of the boys I knew who loved the blues—and, in an irony I've come to appreciate (as a good, middle-class black boy I wasn't allowed to go to the Howard), introduced me to them.

Still, having a foot in both musical worlds meant I sometimes got it from both sides. Black kids demanded I like the Temptations, Ray Charles, and James Brown; white kids expected me to like Motown and the soul music of Stax-Volt and Atlantic (and—they were doomed to be disappointed!—to be able to dance to it). They were confused that I didn't (and couldn't), but at least they didn't make music a test of racial solidarity.

And then along came Hendrix.

He wasn't the first black artist to offer the possibility of a way that was neither black nor white but both. Credit for that goes to Arthur Lee of Love. But Love was, even at the height of its fame, little more than a cult group (its members turned down a chance to play at Monterey), and

Lee (who died in 2006) was too much of a genuine eccentric to become a star.

Hendrix was, well, Hendrix.

It wasn't until I read Ralph Ellison years later, that I discovered how to articulate the possibilities Hendrix created that August night at the Ambassador. Coming to Harlem from Tuskegee in the mid-1930s, Ellison faced a choice—he could hide out in Harlem, the symbolic equivalent of riding the back of the bus in the segregated Alabama he'd just left. Or he could brave the New York subways and learn a new code of manners, going wherever his whims and curiosity took him.

"Freedom," Ellison eventually concluded, "could be grasped only by running the risk of the unknown and by acting in the face of uncertainty," and thus "if I were to grasp American freedom, I was compelled to continue my explorations..."

Ellison was talking, of course, about a particular time and a particular place. And, while it would be years before I read those lines, I understood instinctively that first night at the Ambassador that Hendrix represented the possibility for a kind of freedom that transcended definitions laid down by others.

And the point, in the end, was not to try to become him, but to be like him in being true to oneself and seeking to transcend limits.

what happened that night, after seeing Jimi Hendrix's last gig at the Ambassador, was that I went home. But I almost did get to go to the after-concert party. Someone I knew knew someone else who knew where it was and he told me to stick around—he'd get me a ride there.

After the show, the limousines pulled up to the curb, and Hendrix and the rest of the band got in with the groupies and the hangers-on, and one by one all the limos filled up till there was one seat left. And the guy I was counting on to get me in looked at me and said, "Sorry."

Leaving me to catch the 96 bus down U Street and go home to listen to "Purple Haze" with the speakers pressed up against my ears.

i'll never know what happened at that party and, perhaps, it was better I didn't get the last seat in that limousine.

But in that alternate universe where I did, my lost city where I'm always sixteen, knowing with certainty as sure as the warm sough of my breathing I may grow up but will surely never die, Jimi Hendrix falls asleep on his stomach in Monika Dannemann's London apartment. In the morning, he wakes up with a headache, but picks up the phone anyway and makes the first calls to cut off the leeches who've been feeding on him.

Eventually, the pressure to prove his black bona fides eases and he abandons Billy Cox's plodding bass and Buddy Miles's powerful but unimaginative drumming for musicians who understand the kind of mulatto music that made him famous. He learns to read music, even studies harmolodics with Ornette Coleman himself. He records a series of guitar face-offs that leave Eric Clapton, Duane Allman, and Johnny Winter pleading, "No mas." He collaborates with Gil Evans, records with Miles Davis, finds in Tony Williams the drummer he'd always wanted. With the Kronos Quartet, he records an album for free-form guitar and string quartet. Jazz, rock, and classical music critics call it the best album of the year. It's the summit of his career, they all write. Nothing he could ever do could top it. Until he goes on tour with Sun Ra a year later.

Best of all, with Hendrix to keep them honest, Stevie Ray Vaughn, Ernie Isley, Robin Trower, and all the others find someone else to imitate.

It didn't happen that way, but at least Hendrix was spared the fate of so many other rock legends. Set in a groove, paunchy and balding, they make the rounds summer after summer, playing pavilions and county fairs on the twenty-first century equivalent of the chitlin' circuit.

The truth is, I don't listen to Jimi all that much anymore. I still like to plug in my Strat and crank up the amp to play three-chord blues as loud as my neighbors can stand, but I don't much like listening to loud music.

But when I do put on some Hendrix, I find an elemental fire in his music, a primal quality that reminds me of a hero, armed only with a sword, stalking a dragon in a dark cave, seeking some icon that confers great powers to anyone brave enough to claim it.

"Would it burn me if I touched the sun?" Hendrix asked on one of his songs. It did, alas. It did.

AUTHOR'S NOTE

Not everything happened, but all of it is true.

It would take as many pages as make up this book to thank everyone who offered love, support (and money) over all the years I've been writing.

Jim McPherson, my reason for enrolling at the University of Iowa, was the first writer whose work gave me glimmerings that my particular world might be worth writing about. Bharati Mukherjee encouraged me to keep writing, as did Anton Myrer, Eileen Pollack, Gerald Early, Richard Peabody, E. Ethelbert Miller, Ralph Berry, Stanley Crouch, and many others. Larry McMurtry did too, though surely he no longer remembers the young writer to whom he gave advice one hot summer afternoon in front of Booked Up many years ago.

Thanks also to my colleagues at *The Washington Post* (especially those in *Book World*); to Roger Rosenbaum (the original Deacon Blues); to Susan Coulter; to Cedric Prince for the rap lyric in "Flying Home"; and to Amber Paranick of the Library of Congress for finding W.E.B. Du Bois's 1932 *Crisis* article, "The Secret City: An Impression of Colored Washington." And thanks, finally, to Robert Gossett for making the characters come alive when he read "A Few Good Men" as part of Stories on Stage's "Small Victories" program in Denver. I wrote the story, but you, Robert, had me on the edge of my seat, waiting for what came next.

A former editor and book reviewer for *The Washington Post Book World*, David Nicholson was the founding editor of the magazine *Black Film Review*. He has worked as a journalist for the Dayton (Ohio) *Daily News* and in the San Francisco and Milwaukee bureaus of the Associated Press. He is a graduate of the University of the District of Columbia and of the University of Iowa Writers Workshop. Nicholson lives in Vienna, Va., where he is at work on a biography of A.M.E. Bishop William David Chappelle and a family history/memoir, "The Simonses of S Street: The Story of an American Family."